Broken Pieces

Elissa Daye

This is a work of fiction. Names, characters, places, and incidents are products of the author's imagination or are used fictitiously and are not to be construed as real. Any resemblance to actual events, locations, organizations, or persons, living or dead, is entirely coincidental.

World Castle Publishing, LLC
Pensacola, Florida
Copyright © Elissa Daye 2019
Hardback ISBN: 9781950890026
Paperback ISBN: 9781950890002
eBook ISBN: 9781950560019
First Edition World Castle Publishing, LLC, May 20, 2019
http://www.worldcastlepublishing.com
Licensing Notes
Cover: Melissa Davis
Editor: Maxine Bringenberg

Chapter 1

They say time heals all wounds, but that was a damn lie. Sadie's life was just a reflection of that. Just when she thought she was over it, something else would come back and trigger the past she was trying to shove deep inside her. Some days were better than others, but most were hell to get through, even after all these years. Pretending otherwise was simply fooling herself.

The only consolation she had was her ability to act like everything was perfectly fine, even when the core of her soul felt corroded and stained. The rest of the world, they were easier to manage if they thought Sadie was healthy and whole. Better to think that than to see her as the damaged goods that she had become. She had tried to share her scars with the people who were supposed to care, but she had learned long ago that no one else knew how to navigate the darkness within her. Only she seemed equipped to handle the skeletons, a legacy of a childhood she had never truly had.

Sadie closed her eyes and tried to redirect her thoughts. Every escape mechanism she had was on holiday, and she was left with a mild panic that raced through her veins. After all this time, she was right back where she'd started. Lost, alone, petrified, all because she had been summoned in his name, and while he was no longer a threat, his memory certainly was. The very mention of his name sent thousands of imaginary ants up and down the length of her flesh, immobilizing her like a terrified child. Her stomach twisted and turned painfully, and a hot cold sweat worked its way up her spine as the contents of her breakfast nearly made their way up. Sadie was sure her stomach would revolt at any minute, and she started to look for her escape.

"Ms. Turner?"

Sadie blinked and shook her head. "Yes?" She rose from her chair and took a deep breath.

"Come this way, please." A petite woman with blonde hair gestured for her to follow her.

Sadie walked behind her, alternating between breathing and closing her eyes to shut out the clickety-clack of the heels before her. They reminded her of a ticking time bomb, ready to erupt at any moment.

Sadie attempted to quell the storm of emotions racing through her. Why in the world would they call her back here after all this time? Was he going to manipulate her life from the grave too? Was there no release in death? A tear stained the corner of her eyelid, and she squinted her eyes close together to ward off its tarnished path down her cheek, but the jagged shard cut its way across her flesh. Dashing at it with her hand, she scrubbed the offending liquid away.

Breathe, she told herself. If she could just keep it together for a little while longer, she would be all right. Wouldn't she?

Sadie supposed that depended on what she would learn when she finally learned the terms of her father's will — stepfather, actually. Even though he had been the only father she had ever known, if James Turner could be called that, the man had never learned to be a father, not really. She supposed his own childhood was a precursor to the man he had become, though he rarely ever spoke of it. Her mother often used the rare anecdote to excuse his behavior — well, the behavior she knew about. There were quite a few that were hidden deep inside, so far down it would take an oil rig to dig them out.

"Just inside here, please." The woman directed her through the doorway to a room that was stark in its decorations. White walls — Sadie hated those the most. They reminded her of home. While other people might have thought they were a blank slate, clean and pure, to Sadie they were a shadow of a past she had locked up tighter than Fort Knox, with walls so strong that nothing could break past her defenses.

White walls and hidden skeletons of things no one would ever believe. They never had. Why would now be any different? Not that it mattered. She didn't need to prove herself to anyone anymore. She was safe, successful, and free. Her life was better than she had ever expected it to be. Even so, why did it have to feel like someone had pressed a button and rewound her life back to the time when she had no voice, no control, no way out?

"Have a seat, Ms. Turner." The woman had her hair pulled into a severe ponytail. Her black skirt and starched white shirt accentuated her look, making Sadie feel like a girl inside the principal's office waiting to find out if they would call her parents for some slight mishap.

Mishaps—not that she'd had any of those. Getting in trouble, getting noticed, that would have defeated the purpose of being invisible. There were times that Sadie just wanted to fade away into the background and watch the world turn on its miserable axis. Her only comfort was found inside the safety of the school's brick walls as she learned ways to cope with the turmoil of her youth.

"Do you need anything to drink, Ms. Turner?" The blonde again. Sadie turned to face her with a thin smile plastered on her face.

"I'm good, thank you." Not really. Sadie was far from good. Right now, she'd take a scotch on the rocks to keep her past far away from the forefront of her mind. Unfortunately, that wasn't really a good cure. Sometimes it numbed the pain. Other times it brought it further to the surface.

"Mr. Williams will be right with you."

Williams? Hmmm…she'd known a few of those throughout her lifetime. In fact, her best friend in high school had been Claire Williams. She had lived a few houses down from the small house that Sadie had grown up in. That old Victorian house was still scarred into her brain. Its flaws had been one reason Sadie refused to live in any house that wasn't built in this century.

Sadie was lost in thought when a voice interrupted her from the doorway. "Sadie?"

Sadie looked up and blinked a few times. The man before her was almost familiar, but time and distance had changed him. It couldn't possibly be…. "Justin?"

6

"Yes."

He gave her a charming grin, and Sadie was instantly transported back to her teenage years, when she'd fallen head over heels for his boyish charm. She had never acted on it, though. He was four years older than her, which back then seemed like only a few months — not a big wall to scale at all. Now though, it may as well have been twenty years.

"How have you been, Sadie?"

He looked genuinely interested. His green eyes were as kind as ever, deep enough to get lost in. Sadie wondered how life had kept him in such good graces when it had always seemed to throw her its scraps. Here he was, an attorney, when Sadie had barely made it out of college. Not that she didn't have the brains for it. Her life had just spiraled out of control, often heading at warp speed when she needed a turtle's pace. Her bachelor's degree was enough to land a desk job at Lawson Insurance, where she was one of a hundred drones sitting amidst a sea of cubicles. She spent her days pretending she cared about the people on the other line. Not that she didn't, but most of their anger and hostility with the way things were run was enough to make her want to rip every strand of hair from her head. On the outside, Sadie was rigid like a drill instructor, but just a layer or two beneath the surface she was a ticking time bomb. She feared the emotions that would one day be her downfall.

"I'm fine. Can we get this over with?" Sadie fidgeted in her seat under his scrutiny. Had he heard the bitterness in those two words? *I'm fine.* Sadie was never fine.

"Sure." Justin didn't seem put off by her attitude. He slid into the chair behind the desk and pulled a folder from a drawer. He flipped through a few pages and placed a page before her. "Everything was left to you, Sadie."

"Me? What about Katie?"

"I'm not sure why Katie was excluded from the will, but since your mother passed away, you are the benefactor."

"What if I don't want it?" Sadie's insides were far past twisted. Now they were knotted into tiny pretzels that she would never be able to undo.

"Well...if you want to sign it over to Katie, we could make that happen. But, I will warn you, there is a fair amount of money included with the estate. I would think long and hard before you hand it off to—"

"Katie?" Sadie knew what Justin was trying to say. Katie had been a mess far longer than Sadie. An addict who could not seem to get her own life under control, her older sister was not the best person to hand any kind of money to. It would be gone before the end of the week.

"Well...yes. I think the reason it was left to you was that you were the most stable of the pair of you." Justin's face was like stone, as if he didn't really have an opinion here, but Sadie knew differently.

"I'm sorry...Justin. I know that...." Sadie could not finish her sentence. His own sister, Claire, had an addiction problem that had ended up tearing their family apart. Sadie had lost touch with her long ago. Part of her wondered if they had kept in touch if Claire's life would have turned out differently.

"If you want to have papers drawn up, it will take a little time, Sadie. I suggest you think long and hard about what you want to do before you make a decision. Here are the terms of the will."

For the next twenty minutes, Justin went over the will with her. Her stepfather had left the land, house, and money to her. Perhaps it was his one real act as a parent, but to Sadie it was his last chance to point out that only he seemed to know what was good for her in life and in death. It would seem like a lovely gesture to the rest of the world, a father providing for his child. To Sadie, it felt like he was trying to get his controlling hooks into her one last time. James had always been the master manipulator.

Sadie couldn't help wishing her mother had not died first. Not that Sadie would have wanted much to do with her either. She had chosen that man over her children time and time again. Sadie was pretty sure her mother would still choose him to this day. At least they were together, wherever their souls had ended up.

When Justin was finally done explaining the estate and all that it entailed, he held his hand out to her. "I know this is hard, Sadie. But you will get through it. When someone passes—"

Sadie shoved his hand away. "I hope he rots in hell."

"Sadie...." His eyes filled with concern and slight confusion.

"Thank you for your help, Justin. I'll take your advice into consideration."

Sadie picked up the papers from the desk and stood up. She couldn't stand there in that room one more minute with him. Justin had no idea how much his face reminded her of a past she no longer wanted to visit, even if his handsome smile was part of it. Sadie had many a fantasy of his face when she was a kid. That was almost a lifetime ago. At twenty-six, Sadie

9

no longer believed in fantasies. Sure, she was young, just starting out what should be her adult life, but Sadie had lived like an adult for most of her life, keeping secrets to protect the ones who should have been protecting her. She closed her eyes and let out a slow breath as her hand touched the silver handle of the door.

Sadie turned to the door and then turned back to face him. "I'll be in touch, Justin."

His smile was filled with something that did not register in her foggy mind. "I hope so, Sadie. I really hope so."

"Right."

"Are you staying in town?"

"For the night, I suppose. It's a long road to nowhere from here, you know."

Justin nodded. "I do know."

Did he? Nowhere was a hell of a lot easier to handle than this place. Was it interest that flashed in his eyes, or was he just being nice? Did it really matter? Sadie was going to get as far away from Taylorville as she could. First, she would have to make a few decisions about what to do with the estate and all it entailed. Not that she wanted a damn penny of that bastard's money.

Anger coiled deep inside her and Sadie felt the tears start to rise again. That was the problem with being raised in an emotionally stagnant home—she had never learned how to deal with emotions, the good ones or the bad. Being here, back in the place where it all started, only made her want to shut it out even more. Best plan? Drink her way into oblivion and shove it back down inside the way she always had. First, she'd head back to her room and take care of these papers.

Chapter 2

Sadie opened the door to her room and grimaced slightly. She had forgotten how run down the Tin Roof was. What did she expect from a motel that rented by the hour? On the way up to her room, she'd seen the old gigolo eying her as his next prospect. Sadie shivered as she took in the oily haired toothy grinned man, who thought his assets were on display in the tight jeans that made his ass look like a squished celery stalk. She might not usually have high standards where men were concerned, but there wasn't enough alcohol in the world to turn him into some silver studded cowboy.

Closing the door behind her, she slid the tiny bolt to lock the door, even though it was clearly not strong enough to keep an intruder out. The screws were nearly falling out of the latch. Sadie shook her head. "One week, Sadie. Just one."

One week and she would get the hell out of here and never return. When she met Justin in the morning maybe she could work it out so that he could take over the estate affairs

11

without her presence. She sat down at the makeshift table that was sitting in the corner of the room. It looked like it was constructed from old milk crates or a wooden pallet. Was the economy so low here that they couldn't even afford an actual table? The chair she sat in was rickety, and only three of the legs were straight enough to meet the floor.

She opened her laptop and tried to tap into the closest wireless network. The laundromat down the street had one open for the public, which Sadie found odd. Maybe that was their incentive to keep people doing laundry there? Sadie spent the next hour or two ciphering through her messages from work. She had taken a week off, but Sadie didn't plan on being here that long. If she could get through the estate quickly, she would be home in the next day or so, leaving a handful of days to recoup her senses before returning to work. Nevertheless, she didn't want a pile of work waiting for her on her desk, and some of it she could do remotely.

When she had cleared her task list, Sadie sat up and adjusted her shoulders. Her back popped slightly as her bones settled back into a more comfortable position. Picking up the papers that Justin had given her, Sadie thumbed through them, taking in all the numbers on the pages before her. Two and a half million dollars? How in the world had her stepfather amassed that much money? He was the nastiest penny pincher she had ever met. Growing up, neither she nor her sister had ever seen the inside of a doctor's office — that's how cheap the man was. His threats reverberated in her head even now. *Break one arm and I'll break the other. Stop crying or I'll give you something to cry about.* Those had been his most common creeds. And the worst he'd saved for Sadie herself.

If you tell anyone I'll kill you.

Sadie cringed. Everything in her childhood had been a mass of threats and darkness that was so twisted and cold that she shivered even now. She didn't like to think of herself as a victim. Survivor, maybe. Human, sometimes. Being back in Taylorville just reminded her how broken and damaged she was.

She looked in the mirror and saw the day had worn on her more than she'd thought. Her eyes had dark rings under them, rings she had been familiar with many times. She hadn't slept much at all last night. Sleep had never been her thing, really. She ran a hand through her hair let out an annoyed huff of air.

"Damn it, Sadie. Shake it off," she ordered herself.

"All this money, and very little for the rest of us. What's your game, James?" Sadie never referred to him as Dad anymore. She'd stopped that the minute she left home for good. "Where did this all come from?"

The more she read, the sicker she felt inside. All these years, and not once had her mother ever had a vacation. June had worked her fingers to the bone trying to support their family, while the miser had squirreled away all his money made from various illegal gambling. As far as anyone knew, James was not a very lucky gambler.

Apparently, his luck was something he kept from the rest of them. But why, after all these years, would he even consider giving all his money and assets to her? Was it guilt? Sadie seriously doubted that. The man had been the puppet master where his family was concerned, controlling what they knew and the secrets they kept from the rest of the world, with the ease only a madman would be comfortable with. When Sadie had broken free from his manipulations, his power over the family unraveled. Her older sister, Katie, had left home the minute Sadie had turned eighteen. Maybe she was afraid to go toe to toe with their stepfather without Sadie as a buffer. It would have had more impact had Katie actually left Taylorville. Instead, she had gone from one man to another, picking up one addiction after another while stringing a handful of kids behind her. How many did she have now? Three? Sadie should feel some kind of attachment to them—they were her blood, after all—but what had blood ever done for her? It sure as hell hadn't protected her from the monsters that went bump in the night.

Maybe she should set the money aside for the kids. College funds? Give them a future they didn't have to fight so hard for? Sadie didn't need all that money. Why should she even bother to keep it? She had her studio apartment and a car that worked most of the time. What more could she need from life? Her job was pretty secure, and if she continued to keep herself in check there, she could move up to another position within the company. One that required less contact with the customer base, perhaps? Regardless, Sadie was a survivor. If her job fell through at any point, she knew how to find another one. Determination ran through her bones. She would never be dependent on anyone else.

"All right. So, give the money to the kids. But what if Katie had more?" How would Sadie make sure they were provided for without being involved in the least? Sadie knew she should want to know her nieces and nephews. She only had one sister, but Sadie just could not bring herself to be part of her life. Every time she tried, Katie just blamed her for everything that had ever gone wrong in her life. Sadie had made it a point not to respond to her sister's histrionics. She wasn't trying to be the better person; she simply did not know what would happen if she did confront Katie. Emotions weren't something Sadie was comfortable with having.

"Stay on topic, girl."

More kids. That was still manageable. Sadie would just have to manage the funds from afar. That was really the only way to handle it. As for the house, either she would sell it or hand it over to her sister. First, she would have to make sure it was habitable. Even though she had promised not to return to it, Sadie knew that she had to. She fingered the silver key laying next to the papers and shuddered slightly.

"Best to get this over with." Sadie shivered slightly. "Maybe tomorrow."

Tossing the keys on top of her luggage, Sadie debated what options she had for the moment. Stay in this room, which had hosted who knew how many occupants this week, or find something else to occupy her time. She looked down at the stains that were soaked into the brown faded carpet and wrinkled her nose. It did not take long for her to decide that the less time she spent in this flea-bitten motel, the better. "Out it is, then."

Sadie's phone pinged and she picked it up. A text from her ex displayed across the screen. *Bootie Call?* Sadie rolled her eyes and swiped her finger across the screen. She wasn't going to honor that with a response. That relationship had been doomed from the start. The two had met in a bar, and practically had sex in that same bar that first night. If Sadie hadn't drunk herself into a stupor, she might have come to her senses sooner. Most of their relationship had been like that though—hot, meaningless sex surrounded by an immense amount of alcohol. Neither one had ever been committed to any other person in their lifetimes.

What had she seen in him? He was a means to an end. Her oblivion. No emotions, just sex. That was the only relationship she could tolerate, and it wouldn't change any time soon. There was no happily ever after for her. That only existed in fairy tales written to make women chase after that unachievable castle and Prince Charming. She'd met plenty of princes, and none of them had been charming. At least they had been entertaining. That was something she could use right about now. A bootie call? Sadie giggled. In Taylorville? She'd be the talk of the town by noon. That was the way it worked in small towns. Not that Sadie cared. She wouldn't be here long enough for it to bother her in the slightest.

Sadie walked to the bathroom and tried to look inside the mirror. Several spots were stained on the glass, so ingrained that no amount of cleaning would clean the tarnish off. She did her best to make herself suitable for an evening out. Her brown hair she let fall to her shoulders and brushed it until the curls started to obey themselves. Wavy hair—she should have brought her straightener with her, but she had been so out of sorts when she packed that she was lucky to have a change of underwear. After making sure she was presentable, Sadie was ready to venture out to Taylorville.

Chapter 3

Sadie walked down the street from the hotel, every step filled with a memory she wanted to push away. Not all of them were bad, but the good ones hurt worse. Sometimes it was a reminder of what life should have been like, the life that was stolen from her without a thought. The reverie was a brutality she had tried to bury beneath the surface. Her need for oblivion was outranked by her need to see this through.

She could have walked straight to the Flying Ace bar, but the need to see this world through adult eyes seemed to take over. Walking in the opposite direction, she headed toward Anders Park, the one place she had found sanctuary from her life. Many a night had been spent under the stars, wishing for anything that would take her away from the house that seemed to strangle the life from her daily. She never shared her feelings with Claire, but Sadie always imagined Claire understood why Sadie never wanted to be at home.

Her friend didn't care for Sadie's stepfather at all. If only she truly knew the extent of his disease. Sadie couldn't help wondering if that would have changed her situation at all. What could a child do to save another child? Honestly, no one could have saved her, not when that monster pretended to be the perfect father to the rest of the world. How could one child's voice have changed a thing, when even her own mother had bought into the deceit?

No matter how hard it was to walk with such bitter thoughts wrestling with her concentration, Sadie continued to walk, letting the memories fall like hailstorms around her. When Sadie made it to the park, she sat down at one of her favorite spots from her childhood, the picnic table closest to the woods. Any day she could manage she had spent here with Claire. The two would ride their bikes halfway across town to get there. While Claire probably imagined the fast-paced trek was just for exercise, to Sadie she had been outrunning a demon that followed her everywhere she looked. The world was a much different place back then, when no one feared for the safety of their children the minute they left the house. It wasn't her time away from the house that she had dreaded. It was the time inside.

Funny thing, though—ironic might be a better word. While there had been a big drive to push for children to watch out for strangers, no one had ever warned them of the dangers that lurked closer to home. Sadie should have been able to trust her stepfather. He had been the only father figure she'd ever had, one that wasn't worth the time she spent dwelling on the damage he had inflicted. Usually she was able to keep these thoughts at bay. She had learned how to block them out, to compartmentalize her life so that she never had to deal with his memory again. Being home had knocked the wind out of her sails, though.

Sadie put her head in her hands and tried to still the thoughts circling in her head. She wished she could focus on the moments that had not included the monster in her head, but the moment she had arrived in Taylorville the monster rose from the depths within. Everywhere she looked she was reminded what it felt like to carry a dirty secret in a town where secrets were weapons. Even today, of all days, her defenses were down, letting her past strike her with its deadly venom, destroying the calm she had managed to force over her life.

"Mind if I sit here?"

Sadie almost jumped out of her skin. "Justin! Are you trying to give me a heart attack?"

Justin gave her a cheeky grin, one she remembered all too well. "You always were jumpy."

Sadie looked away. His green eyes were unnerving, even after all these years. Like evergreen in the middle of a snowfall. "If you say so," she grumbled.

"I remember when we used to come here."

Sadie's eyes met his. When had they come here? "I don't remember that."

It was only a half truth. Even back then she had been aware of his every movement, even though she had mastered hiding it. She had not wanted to ruin her friendship with Claire, but she also had not understood the feelings inside her. Sadie had been attracted to him, but that had felt so dirty and tainted, because if she wanted anything with him, had that meant she wanted the other stuff to happen? Sadie closed her eyes briefly and pushed that thought further back, as far as she dared considering the lack of control she currently had.

"My parents used to send me out to keep an eye on Claire."

"Oh, right." Sadie pretended to remember, even though it had been tattooed on her brain long ago.

"I wasn't very good at it, though," he recollected.

"Why's that?"

"I spent too much time watching you instead." His charm suddenly turned up a few notches as he put his hand on hers.

Sadie pursed her lips together and willed herself to pull her hand away. She wasn't one to handle other people in her personal space. While she did have the occasional relationship with men, none of them were ever even close to this intimate with her. She liked her space. It was comfortable. It was hers. Her heart started to beat well on overdrive.

His presence was chasing away the ghosts from her head, even if momentarily. "Claire always hated when you spied on her."

"That's because she knew." His eyes darkened slightly, and Sadie was reminded of a cat ready to pounce.

"Knew what?"

"How much I wanted you."

"Me?" Sadie squeaked slightly. "You can't be...."

Serious? Oh, but he was, which she soon discovered when he leaned closer to her. She felt the warning bells go off, the same ones that kept her guarded from a potential disaster. If he kissed her, would she be transported back in time, huddled beneath the man who had taken every inch of her innocence away? It was a crap shoot every time, but this time Sadie accepted the risk.

His lips were as soft as silk when they glided over hers, like a butterfly landing on the petals of a flower. As he deepened the kiss, Sadie put her hand on his chest, fully prepared to push him away, but her limbs would not comply. Instead, her traitorous hands grabbed his shirt and tried to reach for any tangible piece of him.

She wasn't completely sure if he was actually there. Sadie had dreamt about this moment when she was a teenager. At the time it had made her confused. How could she want to do those things with him, the same things that *he* had done? It was as if ice had been thrown in her face. Sadie pulled away from him in a panic she had been trying to keep at bay. Her heart was racing, and she felt as if all the blood in her body had rushed to her toes.

"Sadie? What's wrong?"

"I can't, Justin." She stood up and walked as fast as her legs could carry her. She didn't get very far.

"What did *he* do to you, Sadie?" He grabbed her arm.

Sadie spun around and faced the only person who had ever bothered to ask. All those years she had wanted to tell someone, anyone who might finally listen to her. But now, before the only man she had ever had any real feelings for, she suddenly felt like sinking to the ground. If only the earth would cooperate and swallow her whole.

"Breathe, Sadie."

She took a deep breath and willed her body to comply. "I can't...."

"Sadie, you can tell me anything."

Could she? He had never been her confidant before. What

21

would he think about her if he knew what James Taylor had turned her into all those years ago? Tears fell from her eyes as a memory entered her mind. A child, lost and alone in a world where the monster was the shadow that entered the room when the rest of the world slept. That shadow made her do things a child should never know.

"He...."

"I knew it." Justin dropped his hand from her arm.

It was then that Sadie knew all her suspicions were true. Telling someone only made it worse. His face was filled with disgust, and the fact that it was at all related to her broke her heart in hundreds of pieces. She felt every inch of her shrivel up and die in that moment. An icy cold entered her veins, as the woman she had become took back over. No more soft, weakness. Time to keep moving as fast as her feet could carry her before the moment got any worse. She was about to sidestep him when she heard his voice break through the fog that had entered her brain.

"I'll kill him."

"Wait, what?" Sadie had already walked about six steps ahead of him. She stopped in her tracks and turned to see the fury on his face.

"That bastard!"

Her eyebrows rose as the rest of her fog disappeared. "You do realize he's already dead, right?"

"Not to you, he's not." His eyes held a compassion that had been missing from her life.

"No." He was right, though. James Taylor's memory was something she had never been able to kill off, no matter how hard she tried. Sadie didn't know what to say. She suddenly

22

started to feel a little light headed.

Justin must have noticed. "When was the last time you ate?"

Sadie look up to the right, a habit she had when she was trying to remember something. "Yesterday?"

"That's it. You're coming with me." He offered his arm to her.

Sadie wasn't sure this was a good idea at all. She had just told him her darkest secret without really saying a word about it. She still wasn't sure how she felt about that. No one else had ever known. While it was her darkest skeleton, it was also a shield that she wielded to keep anyone else at bay. She had dated a few men in her lifetime, but none were the kind of man she would ever have brought home, so to speak. They were simply a means to an end, a nothingness to cancel out the anguish that nearly ate her alive.

"You don't have to do that."

"I want to." His eyes were genuine, something that she was not used to at all.

"Why?" she whispered. When he didn't answer her, Sadie looked down at the ground. "I don't want your pity, Justin."

"It's not pity at all."

She looked up at him and saw the raw desire in his eyes. How could he be attracted to her if he knew the truth? Sadie knew it was a bad idea to go. Any kind of fleeting moment with him would lead to disaster. Unfortunately, the lovesick teen that had been such a part of her still controlled that part of her heart. Sadie took a leap for the first time in forever.

"Okay, but I'm not a fish 'n chips kinda girl."

"Steak 'n potato still good?" He eyed her knowingly.

"Yes."

Sadie couldn't believe that he remembered that. Sadie had always loved a good steak. While other girls were watching their waist in high school, Sadie ate whatever made her feel better. Thankfully, her metabolism had worked well enough to keep the weight off, because stuffing her feelings had been almost too easy to do back then.

"Mind if we leave Taylorville?" He asked her.

Sadie sighed in relief. That was the best thing anyone had offered to do all day. Leaving Taylorville would make it a little easier to sit across the table from him.

"Not at all."

Chapter 4

Justin led her to his truck. Sadie could not help but admire the shiny black luster on its body. Justin had always wanted a truck when he was a teenager. Sadie remembered the first one he got was a fixer upper that had a rust covered frame. She had spent many an afternoon looking out Claire's window as he sanded and buffed that truck into something that actually resembled a vehicle. It was good to see that some things never changed.

"Nice truck," Sadie said when he opened the door for her.

Justin grinned at her. "Yeah, finally got rid of the other one."

"That was a *truck*." Sadie emphasized the word truck, because it was definitely memorable.

"That thing was a beast," he agreed. "But, nothing is worth having if you aren't ready to work for it."

Sadie could not tell if he was talking about the truck, or whether some kind of sexual innuendo was hidden inside that blanketed statement. Normally she would feel flattered, but this was a territory that was unchartered. Other men had said things they didn't mean just to get her attention. Sadie knew that game well. This was not that at all.

"I suppose. Sometimes people tire of the fight though."

"The fight is what makes it worthwhile."

She fought the urge to ask for clarification as she reminded herself she was only here for the week anyway. No need to think about any formal attachment. Sadie had left Taylorville behind a long time ago. It was less than likely she would ever come back once she left this time. Surely he knew that.

"So, where are we heading?"

"Bensen."

"Really?" Sadie had only been there a handful of times before. It was a much larger city than Taylorville, thankfully. "Why Bensen?"

"It's home." He smiled at her.

"Oh, so you don't live in Taylorville?" Sadie was slightly confused. She had just assumed he had returned back home after getting his law degree, although she could not imagine why he would want to return to piddly little Taylorville.

"I don't usually work in Taylorville, except for the odd case here and there."

Sadie almost choked. "So do you find our case odd?"

"No, nothing about you is odd."

Right. Nothing. She begged to differ. Everything that had happened in her lifetime had made her feel less than normal. Was she an oddity? Sadie had always thought so. While she had felt alone most of her life due to the circumstances of her childhood, she had come to realize that more children were

26

abused than anyone ever really knew. Children had no filter, no way of knowing how their world should work, not until they were much older and could rationalize the world with independent eyes.

"Have I said something wrong?"

"What? No...why?" Sadie blinked in confusion.

"You seemed to shut down for a moment." His eyes were filled with concern.

"I'm sorry. I guess I'm preoccupied." Sadie gave him a shy smile, which was out of place for her. With other men, she had been able to push her past aside momentarily. She never let them get close enough to see the cracks in her foundation.

"I can't imagine how difficult this is for you." His voice had the ability to soothe her nerves in ways no one had ever been able to do in the past.

"It is, but it has to be done. It's time to put it all behind me."

"Everything?"

Sadie turned to look at him, and wanted to tell him that there could not be anything between them. They had grown into two different people. But the way he was looking at her made her realize she could not fight the feelings that were stirring inside her.

"We'll see."

He left it at that, thankfully. For the rest of the ride to the restaurant they sat in silence with the radio playing some song or other. Sadie might have recognized some of them if her ears were actually working. Her defense mechanisms were on overdrive as she stared out the window, not really focusing on anything that blurred past her. Much of her life was like

27

that, for she had become a robot, just pushing through. Some people would have searched for a happily ever after. Sadie was not sure that would ever exist for her. Even after all the counseling she had gone through, the darkness seemed to follow her like a shadow she could not shake.

Sadie let out a deep breath that she prayed was inaudible. It was time to switch the dialogue off in her head, time to block it out. She certainly did not want to be a killjoy. If she stayed trapped inside the melancholy, Justin would not want to see her again. Did she want that? Maybe. If only for the time she had here.

As they pulled into the driveway of the restaurant, Justin switched off the radio. "You all right, Sadie?"

His concern caught her off guard. "Me? Yeah. I'm fine."

Fine…that word was a deflection he did not have experience with, not the way she did. F-fucked up, I-insecure, N-neurotic, E-emotional. Just a descriptor she had learned in group years ago. It certainly did describe her current state. Right now she would say she was stuck somewhere between insecure and emotional. Later, that was when she would probably turn neurotic. Someday, maybe the term would change. It had simply been the status quo for so long that Sadie had no other way to define herself.

"You sure?"

Sadie sighed. Would him knowing her past make it impossible to spend any time with him? Was this a mistake? Did he want her to really tell him what she felt? How she thought? Maybe it was better to test the waters now and see how much he really wanted to know.

"You really want to know?"

"I do." His face was somber, as he waited for her to spill whatever feelings she had trapped inside her.

"I…well…." What should she say? No one had really ever asked. "Honestly, I feel like I got ran over by a Mack truck. I'm stuck in a place I thought I would never come back to."

"I can't even imagine." He was sincere, and while the sentiment was nice, she was too jaded to take it seriously.

"Maybe this was a bad idea. I'm a train wreck." Sadie felt tears gather in her eyes, and she wanted to sink into the ground under the truck.

"Sadie, I'm not afraid of a challenge." His hand reached out to wipe away her tears.

"A challenge?" He thought she was a challenge? This was not a challenge. It was a declaration of truth. A reality that no one could change.

"You just need a knight in shining armor to slay all your dragons," Justin stated matter-of-factly.

Sadie tried to be angry with his words. She did not need anyone to save her—she was a grown ass woman, after all. But, the image of him in armor lunging at a mythical dragon with a sword entered her head, and she almost burst out laughing.

"I'm not sure that's possible."

"Anything is possible, Sadie. If you just believe." His face moved closer to hers. "If it's okay with you, I'm going to kiss you again."

Wait, what? Sadie wanted to push him away, to fight the flutter of something dangerous inside her. Hope. She could not get her brain to agree with the raw need for someone to treat her like a normal everyday woman. "Okay…."

29

Before his lips touched hers, he kissed the straggling tears that trailed down her face. Sadie sighed against him when his mouth finally touched hers, like the picture-perfect romantic moment she saw on movies all the time. Sadie had never truly experienced the phenomena before. She imagined that if she were standing on the ground one of her feet would have popped up in the air as she wrapped her arms around his shoulder.

When he broke the kiss, Sadie was speechless. "That was...."

"A start." His words were almost a promise.

A start to what, though? This could only be a moment in time for her. Eventually she would have to return to reality.

Sadie quickly changed the subject. She put a hand on his shoulder and pushed him jokingly. "You promised me a steak."

He chuckled. "That I did."

Sadie did not wait for him to open her door. While it was probably in his nature to be a gentleman, it was Sadie's nature to be independent. She did not need a man to open her door for her. Pushing it open, she slid out of the truck. Hopefully gravity would be kind and her legs would be able to hold her up. That kiss was unlike any she had experienced before. It made her think he must have had plenty of practice over the years.

Sadie looked up at the neon sign on the building. Dusty Broncos. It was not the large establishment she thought it would be. In fact, the more she looked at it, the more she realized it was a hole in the wall place.

"Has this always been here?"

"Forever." He grinned at her as he opened the glass door for her.

"Really?" Not that she would have noticed, because she had only been to Benson a few times before, and it was not like her stepfather ever sprung for a dinner out. But still, Sadie would like to think she would have recognized this place, because they had probably driven by it before.

"Yep. Scout's honor." He held up his hand solemnly.

"Bullshit! You were never a Boy Scout," Sadie snickered.

"Maybe not, but I'm always prepared." He gave her a roguishly handsome smile that made her toes curl.

Sadie did not understand what was happening to her. She smiled at him and shook her head. "You're not prepared for me, Justin."

"But I am." The teasing light left his face and a seriousness replaced it.

"If you say so."

Sadie glanced around the small restaurant and realized why he had chosen it. It was cozy and private. In fact, there were only two other couples inside the restaurant.

"Do we seat ourselves?"

"No, Martha will do that." He nodded to the older woman who was bustling over to them.

"Good evening, Justin. Same as usual?" She winked at him, which made Sadie think she was not the first woman he had brought here.

"Yeah, where is the usual, Justin?" Sadie's right eyebrow rose curiously. Was he squirming?

"Where's Tina?" Martha asked him.

Who was Tina? Was he married? Sadie had not thought

31

to ask. Crap. He could totally be married, 'cause look at him. Why wouldn't he be? Sadie closed her eyes briefly and tried to keep the thoughts in her head at a minimum.

"My *cousin* is spending time with her father," Justin explained.

"That poor kid. Always tossed around from house to house." Martha clucked her tongue like an old mother hen. "This way."

Cousin? She could not believe how relieved she felt with those words. That did not mean that Justin did not have a story to tell. She certainly did not want to start something with him if there was someone else. Start something? Was she doing that? Why would she even go there? Even if they did start something, it would have to be finished by the time she went home. There was no future for them. There never was a future with any of them, only fleeting moments. None of those even compared to the one kiss she had just walked away from.

When they sat down, Sadie saw Justin's knowing glance, which annoyed her. "What?"

"We'll get to that. First, what would you like to drink?"

She was tempted to ask for something strong, but decided water was probably the safest bet. Otherwise, Sadie would make some mistakes that she could not walk away from in the morning.

"Water."

"Same for me," Justin told Martha.

"I'll be right back. Here's a menu for each of you." Martha set the menus down on the table before both of them.

"What do you recommend?" Sadie asked him as her eyes

darted down the menu. Anything to change the topic and keep it that way.

"They make a great sirloin. Nice deflection," he teased her.

Sadie wrinkled her nose and refused to look up at him. He was dangerous, that was for sure. "I'm not deflecting. I'm starving!"

Martha had already returned with their drinks. She had a small notepad and pen in her hands. "What can I get you?"

"An order of skins to start. I'll have a half-rack of ribs, baked potato, and coleslaw," Justin answered her.

"And you?" Martha asked her kindly.

"Sirloin, baked potato loaded, with extra sour cream please. And a side salad with ranch."

"Good choice." She smiled at Sadie. "I'll put this in for both of you. Won't take more than a few minutes to get the skins ready. I'll bring those out first."

"Great. Thanks, Martha." Justin nodded at her before she left.

"She seems nice," Sadie reflected.

"She's been here forever. Her brother is the owner."

"Oh. Nice to keep it in the family, I guess." Sadie did not know what else to say. She took a big drink of water and wondered how she was going to get through this night.

"So, what do you want to know, Sadie?" Justin had already picked up where they had left off.

"Are you married?" She blurted the first thing that came to her head.

"No. Never." He unfolded the napkin before him. "You?"

Sadie choked on her water. "Me? No way."

"No way? Not something you ever want to do?"

"Just haven't been in a relationship worth taking to that level, I guess." That was not the complete truth. Marriage scared the hell out of her. She could barely stand to be in the same space with most men. How would she live with one? "You?"

"Almost. I was pretty serious with a girl in college. I thought we would get married, but it just didn't happen." He swirled the ice around in his glass.

"No girlfriends?" Sadie did not know what had come over.

"Not yet." His eyes met hers, and Sadie almost squirmed in her seat.

"I'm not really looking for anything, Justin." It was the truth. She was not looking for any kind of future. It was too much to hope for.

His eyes challenged her as if to say she would change her mind. "Sometimes the best things are found when you're not looking for them."

"If you say so."

Sadie looked away. She could not afford to get lost in his eyes right now. Sadie had a life to get back to. It wasn't much of one, but it was hers, and she had carved it out of the mountain she had been climbing most of her life.

Justin seemed to realize it was time to change the subject. "So, what do you do?"

"I work at Lawson Insurance. Customer service." Sadie was not really proud of what she did. She was certainly not using her degree to its highest potential. When she had first attended college she had dreamed of running her own business. With her love for reading, she had always wanted to open a small bookstore. Her dream had started to fizzle when the market had become flooded with large retail bookstores. Very few smaller stores remained open these days. If she ever did open one, it would have to be in conjunction with some other business, like a coffee shop or smaller town novelties.

"Doesn't sound that appealing."

Sadie snorted. "Most days I would rather get a root canal."

"Then why are you still doing it?" He asked her.

"Because it pays the bills," Sadie rationalized.

"And if money were not a problem?"

Sadie knew exactly what he was suggesting. "I'm not keeping *his* money, Justin."

"Restitution seems fair," he countered.

"You think it would be restitution? More like prostitution." She slapped her hand over her mouth, and hoped no one else around had heard them.

If he were shocked by her words, he never showed it. "Would you say that to a rape victim getting restitution from her rapist?"

Sadie blinked, and was for once caught off balance. "Well, no."

"You were a victim, too."

"This is not the time or place, Justin." Her cheeks started to blush in embarrassment.

"Everywhere is the time and place, Sadie. Especially when it follows you everywhere."

"How do you know that?" Sadie looked up at him.

"I worked a few cases when I first left law school. It's sickening how many children deal with this, even today."

"Yes. It is." Sadie could not agree more. She changed the topic again. "Do you like being an attorney?"

"It has its moments, like any job. I first started in the city, but did not like the political agendas at my firm."

"Politics aren't my thing either. That's why I just do my job and keep my mouth shut."

As the smell of food wafted closer, Sadie looked up to find Martha bringing the appetizer along with all their food. She was silently thankful. Now they could finish up dinner and he could just take her back to her motel. Then Sadie would try to push the evening to back of her head.

Thankfully, they ate without much more conversation. It was a good thing, because Sadie was actually starving. By the time it was time to go, her stomach was so full that her exhaustion was starting to catch up with her.

She tried to stop a yawn from leaving her mouth. "Oh, excuse me."

"I think it's time I take you home."

Home? Where exactly was he going to take her? "I'm staying at the Tin Roof."

"You're welcome to stay at my house if you like. The Tin Roof is not really a nice place. I live just a few blocks down on Thornton."

"It's what I could afford on short notice. But thank you for the kind offer. If you don't mind, I have a lot to do tomorrow." A lot of things she was dreading too.

"Let's get you back then."

Chapter 5

That night, Sadie's sleep was troubled. Her consciousness seemed to understand she was in for a real battle the next day. As much as she wished she did not have to see the house again, she knew in order to sell it she needed to see how much of its contents needed to be removed. If nothing else, Sadie knew that the ghosts of her past needed to be exorcised from her mind. She had never been able to come home, not once she finally left.

As she pulled up to the house, she was surprised to see she was not alone. Waiting on the porch was the last person she expected to see.

"What are you doing, Justin?"

He made his way down the steps. "Helping you slay a dragon."

"Don't you have work you have to do?" She suddenly felt even more vulnerable.

"I thought if you want someone to handle the sale, an

attorney to work with the realtor, I could offer my services."

Sadie breathed a sigh of relief. Having him here for those reasons was a lot safer than having him try to be her knight in shining armor. She didn't want him to feel like he had to save her from herself. Sadie had been preparing for this moment for years — she just never thought she would have a chance to do it. "That's not a bad idea."

"You ready?"

Yes. No. Maybe. Was anyone ever really ready for something like this? It far surpassed what one might feel heading back to a high school reunion, to a place where they were bullied. It was like visiting the scene of a crime. Yes, it was exactly like that. She shivered as she looked up to the second story bedroom window, the room she had shared with her sister when they were much younger. That was before her sister had abandoned her for the basement.

Sadie turned the key into the lock and took a deep breath. When she pushed open the door, she willed herself to take a step forward. As she did, she was transported back to a time where she had to watch her every step. Sadie felt the vise tightening around her, the manipulative control that had made her feel so trapped within herself.

One step, two. Maybe three or four, and by the time she made it to the living room she saw the chair that her stepfather had refused to get rid of for as long as she could remember. The ghost of him was still sitting there, staring at her with his maniacal eyes, the eyes that he seemed to save special just for her. He wasn't there, but he might as well have been. Tears burned the back of her eyes, and her throat closed as she tried to fight the panic that was rising inside her.

"He's not there, Sadie."

His voice was like a lifeline. It called to her from a million miles away, and she was desperate for it.

"You're right." Sadie shook her head and blinked her eyes a few times.

Anger soon replaced the fear, and Sadie found herself walking to the kitchen before she could stop herself. She retrieved the sharpest knife she could find and made her way back to the living room. Sadie almost felt like a walking zombie at this point, which must have scared Justin a little

"Sadie, what are you doing?"

"What?" She turned to look at him and smiled.

"What are you going to do?" He looked a little worried.

"What should have been done years ago."

The knife arced in the air, and when it hit the old orange fabric she was satisfied with the popping and ripping sounds as she plunged the knife into its depths. That chair, it held so many memories that Sadie needed to destroy every inch of it. The more she stabbed it, the worse she felt though. She dropped the knife and fell to her knees, overcome with grief. Not for the man who had died, but for the child he had killed long ago.

Justin rushed over to her and kicked the knife away. He cradled her in his arms and soothed her with his voice. "Shhh…it's okay, Sadie. You're safe. He's gone."

She stopped crying and laid her head on his shoulder. "I'm sorry."

"Why are you sorry?"

"You must think I'm crazy." Sadie had never felt so wrecked, and she had barely even made it through the door.

She had always thought she would be ready for this. Years of counseling should have built walls strong enough to keep the pain at bay, but the minute the memories circled their acid had corroded any stability she had left.

"I think it takes a strong woman to do what you're doing."

Sadie lifted her head up and sniffled slightly. "Th-thank you, I think."

"My shoulder is pretty strong."

Sadie pushed away from him. There was no way she was going to get lost in those eyes here in this house. "Did Katie come here yet?"

"I don't know. We haven't spoken."

He did not seem put out by her changing the subject at all, which was probably a good thing. Sadie knew her emotions would change faster than the shifting winds. At least with Justin, she did not feel the need to hide them. Oddly enough, his presence was actually more helpful than she'd thought it would be.

"It looks like anything that might have been valuable in this room has been taken."

Likely story. Katie had probably pawned it or sold it to buy more drugs. Her sister was probably feeding her boyfriend's addiction as well as her own. Part of her felt uncharitable with her thoughts, but the truth was hard to ignore. Sadie had tried to help her one time, and her sister had practically talked her out of her college tuition. It was a good thing Sadie had come to her senses before handing the money over to her. Of course, when she had refused to help her, her sister had stopped talking to her and started to blame her for everything that had ever gone wrong in her life,

40

because Sadie was so great and powerful that she controlled the universe. Sadie only hoped she could finish what needed to be done in Taylorville so she could leave and never come back to this place. If she were lucky, she would not even have to come into contact with her sister.

"Do you want to keep any of the furniture?" He asked her as he followed her through the house.

Sadie almost shot daggers at him with her eyes. "Are you serious? Hell no! Is there any place that can use it?"

"Habitat for Humanity often comes in and takes furniture in these types of situations. You could auction it off, too," he answered her.

"I don't want an auction. That will just bring my sister breathing down my neck. Donate it."

Sadie continued to walk through the house, with Justin near her the whole time. She wanted to put a little distance between them, but was glad for the company. Every corner was a different memory. Not an inch of the house was free from the darkness, but having him there was like a buffer. She did not have to face it alone, and she was more thankful for that than she would ever be able to vocalize.

When she made her way up to the room that had been hers, Sadie was thankful that none of the furniture was in place. Here it looked so small and empty. That was the way she needed it to be. The only thing that caught her attention was the blinds that covered the windows. She stood there staring at them, as if stuck in a trance. It was in fact a pattern she had learned a long time ago. The zig-zag of the cord strings as they threaded through the plastic slats was something she had tattooed in her brain. Many hours had been lost counting the number of slats, memorizing every fleck of dust as she tried to ignore the life that was happening around her. It was easier to block it out if she focused on that one thing.

Justin must have noticed the impact, for he walked over to the window and stood in front of it. "Look at me, Sadie."

Still she looked past him as flashes of images flooded her eyes. No matter how hard she tried, Sadie could not break free from it. Barely breathing, she was hypnotized by the terror that had been trapped inside her for so long. Justin turned away from her and ripped the blinds from the brackets, then tossed them to the ground. In that moment, the spell was broken.

"Sadie, look at me."

His voice was gruff, and filled with an emotion she could not place. Was he mad at her? Sadie was afraid to look at him. Rather than look at him, she stared at her feet.

"Sadie, please look at me." The coaxing timbre of his voice crossed the distance and made her realize he was there to help her. "He's not here, Sadie."

"No. He's not." She felt a shiver run up her spine.

"Do you want to get out of here?" he asked her.

"Yes." It was a whisper that left her mouth before she even thought about it.

"Let's go." He held his hand out to her and she reached for it.

It was the first time she had ever held another man's hand, and she didn't second guess it. As they left the house, Sadie locked it behind her and made herself a promise to never return. She didn't care what happened to it. While seeing it one last time had been hard, there was a part of her that knew conquering the fear was a battle she'd had to fight. The battle had not gone the way she thought it would—Sadie had always thought she would be strong enough to face it without breaking down—but the truth was some things she would never be over. That did not mean she had to put herself in a situation like this again, though. This house could burn to the ground for all she cared. It still would not erase the pain that she tried to keep tucked away neatly like hospital corners that never seemed out of place.

"How much would it cost to pay you to deal with the realtor on this?" Sadie asked him as they walked down the steps.

"Just the standard fee, Sadie. Hell, I'd do it for free even."

"No, I'll pay the fee, please." It was her need to stand on her own two feet that refused the kindness he offered.

"Very well, Sadie." He sighed slightly.

"I will let you take me to lunch though," Sadie threw out to him.

"Oh, you're on." He grinned at her.

"I just need to get the dust off me. Can I meet you somewhere?"

"Mexican?" suggested Justin.

"Sounds good. Text me the details and I'll join you there."

"I can pick you up if you like."

"Sure. That works too." Sadie did not mind if he escorted her around town. That would probably be easier than trying to navigate around her memories.

"Noon?"

"Sounds good. I'm in room 112."

Sadie opened her car door and slid into the seat. She was

thankful that she had the door separating her from him. Her emotions were still raw, and she wasn't quite sure how to deal with the concern chiseled across his face. She would have a few hours to regroup, a few much needed hours.

Sadie knew she should feel the trauma of the moments earlier, but it left as soon as it came. The rawness was still there, but the minute she stepped out of the house, she had closed a chapter in her life that had been open for far too long. She was reminded that she did have coping mechanisms that worked, and that she had known it was going to be hard to come back here to where it all happened. From here on out, that house would cease to exist for her. Sadie was moving forward, in whichever direction that happened to be.

She knew what direction her heart wanted to move, but her brain was having trouble negotiating the proper terms. Justin. She had no idea how she was going to make that work, especially considering the distance between them, emotional and physical. He seemed so down to earth, put together, and, well.... She was often split at the seams with emotions she could never seem to control. That was why she shoved them as far inside as she could. It was better to not react to the world around her. If she could keep everything organized in every area of her life, make all the pieces fit in the right places, then she could breathe. Somehow, she knew having any kind of relationship with Justin would shake up all the pieces and send her spiraling into the unknown.

Did Sadie want to know what was on the other side of it all? Sometimes. All she had known up to this point were men who were only interested in a casual relationship, sexual encounters that really had no substance. Those were the only

44

kind Sadie had ever been comfortable with, because the other kind meant she had to feel. Sadie was terrified of that more than anything. Yet, here she was imagining what life could be like if she had that with him. Was that even possible?

Chapter 6

Sadie had barely made it back to her room when a knock sounded on the door. She smiled as she opened the door. "You're earl—"

"So you got everything?"

Sadie gasped when she saw her sister standing in the doorway. This was the moment she had been trying to avoid. "Katie…."

"What did he leave you?"

"Well, you look well." Sadie was lying through her teeth, though. The gaudy makeup that Katie had painted on her face made her look like a hooker on a bender. If this was her day makeup, Sadie hated to think about what her night look was.

"Are you going to invite me in?" Her stringy blonde hair looked as if had not been washed in weeks.

"Here? Sure, I guess." Sadie wanted to tell her no, but her defenses were still down.

"Well, I would have thought you'd pick the Hilton." Katie

scrunched her mouth together in distaste.

"Taylorville doesn't have a Hilton," Sadie countered. Not that she would have ever stepped foot inside one. She didn't spend her money so frivolously. Not that Katie would believe her.

"So, did the old man leave you anything? You always were his favorite," Katie accused her.

"No, I wasn't." Sadie's insides started to churn.

"Yes, you were. You always got to do everything. I always got the short end of the stick. Maybe if he had loved me as much as you, I wouldn't be where I am today." Katie inspected her fingernails.

"Really?"

"Oh, don't start with the abuse thing again. No one believes you. Mom never did either."

Sadie screamed silently inside, knowing that if she opened her mouth she would never stop. "You told Mom?"

"Yeah. It broke her heart that you wanted to spread such malicious lies."

"I didn't spread a lie. The only person I ever told was you."

That had apparently been a mistake. Sadie had been in a low point, and reached out to her sister when she had left the house. With Katie out of the house too, she had wondered if her sister had been abused as well. She remembered that phone call to this day. Her sister had laughed aloud as if Sadie had lost her mind, and told her that she was imagining things, that her imagination had always been overactive.

"I sincerely doubt he ever did anything to you."

"Why, because you didn't see it? Well, good for you. So

47

glad I could spare you the trauma."

"Trauma? You wouldn't know trauma if it slapped you in the face. Now, me, I got the worst of it from that man. Nothing I ever did was right. He never had a kind word for me. Maybe if he had cared for me the way he did you, I wouldn't be stuck where I am. It's all your fault."

"My fault?" Sadie felt the blood drain from her face.

"You had all his attention." Katie sneered at her.

"So, let me get this straight. If he had not spent so much time on me, your life would have been better." There were words inside her that she wanted to scream at her sister, but she knew reasoning with a drug addict would not accomplish anything.

"Yeah."

Sadie was shaking with anger. It was always unreasonable to think her sister should have protected her, she knew that now. But it was not unreasonable for her to expect human decency from her right now. She let the words fly, everything she had always kept bottled up she flung at her sister. "You think I wanted him molesting me? No, fuck that. Raping me. Do you think I am any less screwed up than you?"

"He never laid a hand on you. You're delusional. I'm glad Mom's not around to hear this."

"Say whatever you need to help you sleep at night, Katie." Sadie realized that any other outbursts would only be damaging to herself. Katie was well past any empathy for anyone but herself.

"How much money did he leave you, Sadie?"

"Why?" Sadie waited for her to sink the dagger in her back even further.

"I have some bills to pay." Katie looked away from her, and Sadie knew her sister was lying to her.

"Do the kids need anything?" Even now, she tried to give her sister the benefit of the doubt.

"What kids?" Katie asked her.

"Surely your brain isn't that fried. Your children, Katie. There are three, right?"

"I don't have children anymore," she answered matter of factly.

Had she killed them? They were not something you could just misplace. What did she mean she didn't have kids anymore? "What are you talking about?"

"The state took them and I gave up my rights. I have no idea where they are. The records are sealed."

"Why?"

Sadie could not imagine why anyone would just give up their kids without a fight. Then there was the thought that had always popped her in her head. If her sister could not afford children, she should not have had them in the first place. It was not anyone else's responsibility to clean up her messes, but apparently it was. Sadie should feel sad that she would never know Katie's children, but she remained numb about it, just like usual. She couldn't miss something she'd never experienced.

"Why did you let them go?"

"It was that, or go to jail. It's for the best, really." Katie rolled her eyes. "They were cramping my style. Did you get any money or not?"

Sadie blinked. Was that all she cared about? Clearly, Katie did not care about anyone but herself. In a matter of seconds,

49

she had gone from her telling her that she'd lost her kids to asking for money. What was wrong with that woman? Was she that entitled? Did she even know how hard the rest of the world worked to support themselves? And here she was looking for a handout that she had never earned. Sadie knew now that she could not let the money go to her sister. As much as Sadie didn't want to take it, she knew that it would only make Katie's life worse. She would spend it faster than a kid in a candy store. Nothing would change.

"Get out."

"What?" Katie looked at her as if she'd lost her mind suddenly.

"Get out. Right now."

"At least give me the house."

"Why? So you can turn it into a drug den? I don't think so." Sadie would donate the house before she would let that happen.

"How dare you!" Katie sucked in her breath.

"You'd be surprised at what I'd dare, dear sister. Now, get out or I will call the police."

Sadie knew that trying to force her out of the room herself would not give her the result she wanted. She was likely to get in a fist fight with her before the incident was over. Sadie was not in the mood for that, and there was no way her sister would be prepared for the rage that boiled inside her.

"Fine, but you haven't heard the last of me. I'll get an attorney and fight you for the estate," threatened Katie.

"You do that." Sadie was not afraid of the fight, mostly because Sadie knew Katie didn't have the money for an attorney. Not many would take on a drug addict either. She'd have to scrape the bottom of the barrel.

As Katie left, Sadie locked the door behind her. She picked up her phone and sent a quick text to Justin. *Rain check?*

Sadie was now in fight or flight mode. She started to pack her things, knowing that she could not spend another second in this town. The more she thought about it, the more she wanted to disappear from anywhere anyone could find her and head into oblivion, where she could forget anything that mattered. Now, she wished she had thought to stock the small fridge with something strong, but drinking would only numb the feelings for so long.

Her phone dinged and she looked down at the message. *Negative. I'm coming for lunch.*

Sadie sighed. He was going to be one disappointed man when he realized Sadie had left, but she could not think about that right now. She had to get out of here as quickly as possible, and letting him shift her narrative was not going to fix the problem. Sadie did a double check and made sure that everything she'd brought with her was in her trunk. Turning in her key, she settled her balance and left before she could second guess herself.

At twelve, her phone dinged again, but Sadie did not turn it over. She didn't need to look to know that Justin was asking where she was. Instead, she kept driving as far and fast she could, knowing that she would only feel safe when she returned to her small studio apartment, far away from the world that spun her upside down and inside out so mercilessly.

Five hours later, Sadie turned the key in her lock and pushed the door open. Switching on the light, she took a deep breath, hoping that her thoughts would start to slow down and she could return to normal. Everything was exactly in the place where she had left it. She set her bags down on the floor and walked over to the couch, where she finally glanced at the messages on her screen.

12:10. Where are you?

12:40 Are you okay?

1:00 Your car is gone. Did you leave?

2:00 Did I do something wrong?

2:30 I'm here if you want to talk.

3:00 Please don't shut me out.

3:15 Call me if you want to talk.

4:00 Let me know you're all right.

4:30 I care about you.

Sadie blinked. Why did he care so much? They had only shared a dinner and a few kisses. And well, her private hell. She hadn't meant to shut him out—or had she? He was as much a threat to her as her sister. Where her sister was a walking tornado set to destroy everything in her path of destruction, he was much worse. The promise of something more was devastating. Sadie had never thought she deserved the kind of world he wanted to show her. She just wanted to survive in her present life without anyone disturbing the order she had within it.

But there was a problem with that philosophy. The life she lived had always suited her. She had never known better, never found a man she felt could understand the cracks in her smile and see the emptiness she hid deep inside her. Could he? Wasn't it worth exploring?

"Damn it, Sadie!" She cursed herself. Why did she always

feel like she was making the wrong decision?

Ten minutes later, Sadie found herself in her car for the second time that day, making a trip to a place that was even more disturbing than the one she'd left, because she had no idea what would happen when she got there. Fighting the fear, she made herself follow through. She had to know what was on the other side.

Chapter 7

Hours later, Sadie stood outside Justin's door. She remembered him telling her that he lived a few blocks down from the restaurant. The mailbox had his name on it too, unless it was another Williams. Sadie pressed the doorbell, half afraid he wouldn't answer, and even more terrified that he would. What was she thinking? She was about to turn around when the door opened.

"Sadie! Thank God!" The relief in his voice was palpable. He had the look of a man who had not slept in days, but she had only been gone for a few hours.

"I'm sorry." Her chin wobbled slightly as the words broke through her lips. She did not know what else to say.

Justin pulled her into his arms and stroked the top of her head. "It's okay, Sadie. Shhhh."

His words broke the dam that had kept everything in a neat order in her life, the control over the emotions that were always rocky just beneath the surface. She barely noticed him gently coaxing her inside as the tears streamed down her face. It was like a lifetime of grief came pouring out.

"I'm sorry…. I know it's late. I—"

"Sit down, Sadie." He ushered her to the couch in the living room.

Sadie sat down, but she did not let her body sink into it very far. She sat on the edge, her knees clenched as close together as possible. Her arms wrapped around her stomach as she fought the urge to rock back and forth on the couch. She felt like the child trapped in her room, rocking herself back and forth as she cried silently in the corner in the dark.

Justin waited until the tears almost stopped before he spoke. "Did something else happen?"

"Katie…."

"Shit!" Justin let out an irritated breath. "I was hoping she would know better than to show her face near you."

Sadie looked down at the floor. "It's all about her. It always has been. She doesn't believe a word I said."

"I believe you." His words were a soft whisper across a desolate desert.

"Why?" Sadie looked up at him, truly wondering why he believed her so whole-heartedly when her own flesh and blood was in such denial.

"You're not a liar, Sadie. No one can manufacture that kind of grief." Justin moved closer to her on the couch, as if gauging what kind of distance was appropriate in this situation.

"You're too good to be true." Sadie saw him in front of her, with the sweet gentle concern that she had always yearned for deep inside, but she wasn't sure how to digest it.

"I'm imperfect, Sadie. I'm just as flawed as anyone else."
He held his hand out to her and she latched onto it.

"I hate Taylorville. I hate my life. I hate…." She looked up
at his face. She wanted to say she hated feeling the way she
did, but the words never vocalized.

"What do you hate?"

"Feeling. Not feeling. Being alone." The quiet, the silence,
the emptiness. Sadie wanted to ask him for more than any
man had given her, but how did she voice that which she did
not understand? What if Sadie had no idea what she wanted?

"You're not alone." His finger ran along the lines of her
palm, and Sadie shivered slightly.

"Why do you care so much?" Sadie wondered aloud.

Her question seemed to stump him. He looked as if he
were debating the right answer, or the one that would not
send her flying out the door. "Because you need me."

She needed him? How did he know that for sure, when
she didn't even know what she was really doing here? Every
inch of her still wanted to run, but the promise of something
brighter than the darkness that surrounded her was too much
to pass up.

"What if I can only give you moments?"

"I'll take whatever I can get, Sadie." His hand moved up
to caress her cheek softly.

"No strings?" She almost retracted the words the minute
they left her mouth. What if she did want strings? What if she
wanted to spend the rest of her life wrapped in his arms?

"None at all."

His answer was not the one she really wanted. To her it
meant he only wanted the here and now. Sadie was afraid

to wish for more, for it did not fit nicely into the life she had carved for herself. Regardless, Sadie was too smart to turn down whatever he was willing to give. She was mere inches from kissing him on the mouth, but the fact that there was very little space between them made her start to panic slightly. He seemed to understand.

"Have you eaten?"

"Eaten?" Sadie blinked. With the time she had spent on the road since this morning, she had barely eaten a candy bar.

"I'll take that as a no. Let's change that now." Justin stood up and walked from the room.

Sadie, curious by nature, decided to follow him. As she did, she took in the stark surroundings of the house. Everywhere she looked the walls were covered in a bland khaki color that made her think Justin had never redecorated from the time he moved in. Realtors were big for painting everything neutral. It made for a blank canvas for any potential buyers. There were a few black and white photos of nondescript places hung down the hallway. A flower, a tree, a river and mountain, things that reflected his love of nature. At least that was what Sadie assumed.

His house did not reflect his career path. Sadie was fairly sure he could have afforded a much larger house, but Justin was living the life of a bachelor. His two-story house was big enough for him to spread his things out and be able to breathe. The kitchen was large enough to make a small feast, certainly larger than any that Sadie had ever used.

"Nice kitchen."

"I like to cook," he grinned at her.

"I can see that." Sadie smiled. Justin had already started

to pull some things out of the refrigerator—thankfully they were leftovers. She did not mean to make him go to so much trouble for her. "A sandwich would be enough. Seriously."

"Can't have you fading away on me, Sadie. Besides, a full stomach will help you get some sleep. You look like you could use some."

Sadie looked down at the floor. "I don't sleep much."

"You just need the right circumstances." Justin continued to piece her plate together and put it in the microwave.

What circumstances were those? Sadie would be more than happy to experience those if it meant she could actually feel rested. No matter how much sleep she got, she always woke up exhausted. Then she crammed in enough caffeine to help her function for the day. Most days were long, but Sadie managed to get through. Today was one of the longest she'd had.

As the food started to heat, Sadie's stomach started to grumble and she became light headed. "Maybe skipping food was a bad idea."

"Maybe you should sit down." He nodded to the kitchen table.

"Good idea." Sadie walked over to the table and pulled one of the chairs out before sitting down.

When he brought the plate of lasagna to the table, he broached the topic they had avoided so far. "So...when I went to the motel you had checked out."

"Yes." Sadie did not know what else to say. She ran?

"So, am I right to assume you need a place to stay?" His eyes looked almost hopeful.

"Um...yeah. I guess I should have asked if that was okay

before I just—"

"It's okay, Sadie. I have an extra room. You're welcome to it any time." He pushed the parmesan cheese closer to her, then stood up to make her a drink.

Extra room? Her spirits sunk slightly. She was hoping that...well, she wasn't all too sure what she had been hoping for, but the thought of sleeping in the same house with him, the way she had when she was a teenager, was unsettling. She wasn't a little girl anymore; she did not want the rooms to separate them. But maybe he didn't want what she wanted.

She did the only thing she could do under the circumstances. "Thank you."

"How long have you lived here?" She asked after she ate a few bites of her food.

"Two years."

She watched him as he swished his glass in front of him. He was drinking something stronger than water—she could smell the alcohol. Brandy? Bourbon? She wouldn't mind that herself, but he had only given her water. Maybe it was better that she didn't drink. Every part of her wanted to lose herself inside his arms, but at the moment, they did not seem to be on the same page about that.

"It's nice."

"Three bedrooms, two baths. More than enough room for me."

"Much bigger than my studio apartment. It's nice. You've done well for yourself."

"You'll be able to afford your own place if you want it," he reminded her.

"I guess so. Maybe I'll just invest it." Sadie was still not sure what to do with the money, but that wasn't something she had to decide right now.

"So, how long are you off work?" He asked her.

"I took the week off. I haven't decided what to do with my time." Her eyes met his and she almost shivered. He did want her — she knew the signals. But he wasn't pushing anything. The easy banter back and forth between them was like a cordial dance. Sadie hated it. She wanted to feel something more, but could see how exhausted he looked. "I'm keeping you up. I'm sorry. You must have work tomorrow."

"I have a deposition in the morning." He looked as if he were stifling a yawn.

Sadie pushed her food away from her. She'd eaten enough to take the edge off her hunger. Anything more than that and she might spend the night on the toilet. Her nerves had taken over far too long today. "I could use some sleep too."

Sadie stood up and took her plate over to the sink. She scraped the excess into the garbage disposal and looked for the switch. She turned to ask him where it was, but found him standing right in front of her. "Where's…?"

She barely got that word out before Justin pulled her into his arms. His mouth was on hers before she had a chance to think. She thought back to all the times she had wanted to do just this, and heat filled her face. He pulled her closer to his body, and she felt the muscles buried beneath his clothes. Sadie longed to run her fingers over them. She wrapped her arms around his neck and clung to him as his mouth continued its serenade against her mouth.

His mouth left hers and started to rain kisses down her cheek, to the curve of her neck, to one of the most vulnerable spots on her body. Every inch of her started to tingle with desire, and she sighed against him. His hands massaged her back as he continued his assault. Every inch of her came alive in a way it had never been before, and when he pulled away from her, she was left aching for more.

When her eyes met his she could see the conflict inside. He brought her hands up to his lips and kissed one at a time. "Your room is already made up, Sadie. Second door on the right at the top of the stairs."

Sadie watched him walk away and wanted to call after him. Why would he kiss her like that and just walk away? Was something wrong? He seemed to be enjoying the encounter as much as she had. Or was that just for show? Sadie fell back into her normal pattern of second guessing everything that happened around her. She waited until she heard a door close upstairs before she went out to get her things from her car.

The fresh air hit her face and she breathed it in. Cold. October. It used to be her favorite time of year. The smell of leaves as they clumped together in piles on the ground. The pumpkin spice that really teased the taste buds, alluding to the pies that would soon follow in November. Memories were haunting pieces, things she could reach out and almost touch. The good ones never stayed around long enough to make a difference. Sadie shivered slightly as she pulled her bag from her trunk. She let herself back into the house and figured out the locks on the door so she could lock up for the night.

As she made her way up the stairs, she saw the faint glow of a light under a door to the left. Justin. She longed to push the door open and seek solace in the man inside, but it was like a visible line had been drawn on the floor between them.

Opening the door to the guest bedroom, she walked in and shut it quietly behind her. Tears gathered in her eyes, the excess of everything that had hit her during the day. None of it hurt as much as Justin pushing her away.

"Nothing is ever easy," she whispered aloud as she started to pull out her sleepwear, a large T-shirt that hung down to her knees.

Turning off the light, she walked back to the bed. She pulled back the covers and slid beneath them. The sheets were cool to the touch as she settled inside them. Usually she preferred the cold against her skin, but her body ached for a warmth that was denied. She closed her eyes and tried to fall asleep.

Chapter 8

The minutes ticked by slowly, as the clock on the wall seemed to echo louder than the beat of her heart. Sadie tossed and turned, unable to ignore the thoughts racing through her head. To be so close to the object of her desire without acting on it was killing her inside. He was trying to be the nice guy, but Sadie didn't want a nice guy. Not right now. She wanted so much more than that. The more she thought about the kiss downstairs, the more her heart seemed to race. She throbbed in places that should be dormant, especially if she was supposed to go to sleep.

Sadie sat up in bed and decided to throw caution to the wind. "Screw it."

When she opened her door, her breath caught in her chest. Justin was standing right outside, running one of his hands through his hair. He was fighting the same tumultuous battle she was. She stepped past the doorway and pulled his face down to hers. His lips were soft and sweet against hers,

63

but she felt the torture behind him.

He pulled away from her and put a hand to her face. "I shouldn't—"

"I'm not going to fall apart, Justin." That might not be the exact truth. Being with him had the ability to rip away her sanity. Sadie was not sure what would be left over when he was done.

"You've had a long day." His excuses were valid, yet their logic taunted him. His face showed how much he was torn between doing the right thing and doing what his body clearly wanted.

Sadie knew he was concerned with her fragile state of mind. The fact that she had visited her living hell today probably made him want to run himself, she was so screwed up. Any man would have run a long time ago, closed the door and walked away. It would not have been the first time. But not Justin. He was still here, standing in front of her taking up the gauntlet, ready to slay any dragon for her. Sadie did not deserve him.

"You've had a long day too." Sadie threw out a life raft, his way out before disaster erupted before him. She waited for him to take it, but he did not budge.

"I'm not tired."

He lied. Justin was tired—Sadie would have to be blind not to realize that. It was almost midnight, and he had worked all day after walking through the house with her. Sadie knew how draining that had to be for him. Sadie regretted that. She never wanted to be someone's project, something to fix, for she had always prided herself on taking care of herself. Letting others do so was a sign of weakness, one she refused to give in to.

At least she had until Justin Williams came back into her life. Looking down at the floor, she suddenly wished it would swallow her whole. She stood before him, awkwardly awaiting the decision that would define the rest of her life. She was not kidding herself that this would actually lead somewhere, but she knew that one night with him would be better than any of her sexual encounters with anyone else. She trusted him.

"Maybe, I should just—"

Justin cut her off. "I want you, Sadie."

"I want you too." More than she had ever wanted anything in her life. She did not remember most of her encounters—she barely stayed present in the moment—but with Justin she wanted to remember every single moment. If she could tattoo it in her mind, it might carry her over to the rest of her life.

His mouth covered hers, her words all he needed to hear. He moved her back with him, one step at a time, not once coming up for air. By the time he broke the kiss, Sadie was breathless with anticipation. His mouth continued to work down her face, while his hands slid under her shirt. As his fingers moved up her back, she reveled in the heat they brought to her skin. His mouth moved down to her neck and Sadie moaned softly. His hands brushed against the curve of her hips as he pulled her against his body. She felt the hard erection bulging through his pants, and whimpered as she thought how nice that would feel inside her.

Sadie wanted too much too fast. The words escaped her lips before she could retract them. "I want you."

He growled against her skin. "I feel like a randy teenager."

65

Sadie giggled. "Well, there is no one to keep you from living out your fantasies."

"No parents here?" He asked her jokingly.

"No. Oh...what are you doing?"

Sadie almost jumped away as his fingers slid into the front of her panties to stroke between her legs. The more he stroked, the hotter her face started to feel. His handiwork stripped her of any sane thought as she throbbed against his finger. She clutched his shoulders and almost fell backwards when one of his fingers slipped inside her.

"Reality is so much better," his hot breath whispered in her ear, right before his teeth caught the bottom of her lobe.

In that moment, every inch of her came unhinged as the first orgasm rippled through her. "Oh...ah...."

His mouth trapped hers in a hungry kiss, swallowing her next exclamation as he continued to work his magic. Sadie almost collapsed against him, but he held her up easily. His fingers released her and he slid her underwear down her legs. "So wet."

Sadie shivered when his hands pushed the shirt over her head. His sharp intake of breath when he ran his fingers over the scars on her legs made her want to push him away. He leaned down and kissed each one of them, seeing them as more than just scars. Tears sprung to her eyes and she tried to keep them at bay. Sensing her predicament, Justin stood up and caressed her cheek.

"Never again, Sadie."

"That was a long time ago...." More like six years ago. That was the last time she had cut. When she was safe from harm, she had learned to stop destroying herself. She usually kept her scars hidden, which was why even in her most intimate moments, she kept her distance. Here she was revealed and raw, open for him to see. She should feel disgusted, but his gentle touch made her feel endeared, protected.

"Good."

While Sadie had feared the moment was gone, that Justin no longer wanted to continue, he surprised her by lifting her up in the air and carrying her to the bed. He tossed her down on the bed and gazed down at her. "Just as I imagined."

"Oh?" Sadie's eyebrow rose curiously. "And just what did you imagine?"

"You in my bed. Naked."

"Well, I'm here. What are you going to do about it?" She could see most of his body at this point. He definitely worked out. His chest was hard, defined, from the rock-hard abs all the way up to the firm nipples that jutted out of his muscled chest. How she longed to run her fingers over his body, to feel his hot skin on her own, but Sadie would have to wait.

When he took his pants off, Sadie nearly lost her mind. He was well endowed. She had always imagined he would be, but fantasy was nothing compared to reality. Another first for her. Sadie never looked at a man's parts—she barely even touched them. It was just not in her nature. Then again, none of the men she had slept with made her want to lose her mind in just a matter of seconds, not like Justin.

"Like what you see?" he teased her.

Sadie blushed and looked away. She had never really stared like that before. She felt the bed move next to her. His hand touched her cheek.

"Don't look away, Sadie. I want you to see me. There's

nothing to be ashamed of here."

Sadie smiled at him. "You're pretty sure of yourself."

"Nothing is ever a sure thing. Are you sure you want to do this?"

Sadie fought nervous giggles when his hand moved down her stomach. "Yes. I want to."

She marveled at his gentleness. No man had ever asked her if she was sure before. She had always just gone along with it. Justin understood her better than anyone she'd ever met before. His hands roamed all over her body, while their eyes remained locked together. She saw the desire growing in his, and knew he felt the same burning coils inside that she did.

Sadie knew he was holding himself back. She pardoned him with her next words. "I want you *now*, Justin."

He groaned. "I've imagined this for so long."

His hands parted her legs and he rose over her. When he slid into her, she felt he was the piece she had always been missing. As he moved up and down, Sadie kept her eyes trained on his. He reached down and kissed her mouth, and she felt the fever rising inside her again. The faster he moved, the closer she came to oblivion. When her finish came, she closed her eyes and rode waves. As she quivered around him, she felt him stiffen and push harder into her. The rhythm he set created an eruption she had not planned. By the time he finished over her, she was still seeing stars.

He looked apologetically at her. "I'm sorry."

"For what?" She blinked at him in confusion.

"I might have been just a tad worked up."

"Oh?" She had not really noticed. For the first time in

forever, she had only been focused on how she felt in that moment in time.

"Teenage dream meets reality."

"How did it measure up?" She asked him.

"Nothing could compare to the real thing."

Sadie yawned. "It was pretty good."

"Looks like I've managed to put you to sleep," he chuckled.

"What? No. I'm just exhausted." Sadie started to sit up, to go back to the room she had just walked out of, but Justin pulled her into his arms.

At first, Sadie did not know what to do. In all her relationships, not once had she ever slept in another man's arms. It was always "Wham bam thank you ma'am, now get out." Sadie put her hand on his chest and let herself melt into his warm body. With her head on his chest, she could hear the steady beat of his heart. Her eyelids fluttered up and down, and she fought another yawn. Justin pulled the covers up around her and pulled her even closer. She heard him sigh, and his own breathing started to change. She fell asleep to the rise and fall of his chest and the warmth of his embrace.

Chapter 9

When Sadie woke up, she was surprised to find it was well past her normal waking hours. Justin was not in sight. At first she wondered how he could just leave her alone like this, but then she remembered he had an early morning deposition, one that she had completely distracted him from, so she could not be too upset with him.

She stretched and yawned, and realized she was still naked under the covers. Sliding the covers away from her body, she quickly searched for the T-shirt that had been strung carelessly on the floor. When she found it by the door, she remembered that he had undressed her there. Her hand ran over the scars on her legs. He had told her never again, as if he had realized the wounds had been self-inflicted. She knew the topic would come up again — it was inevitable. Justin was too observant to skip over it.

Sadie scooped up her shirt and slid it down over her head. She slid her panties on and took a deep breath. Opening the door, she looked left and right as she crossed the hall. She wasn't sure exactly what time it was as she went to the guest room to retrieve her phone.

"9:00?" Sadie blinked in confusion. Had she slept in that much? Was it the exhaustion of the day? The release of endorphins? Or the comfort of his arms? All three? Sadie could not remember the last time she had slept so well. No bad dreams, no cold sweats. No monsters hiding in the corners. She had felt safe and loved for the first time in her life. Not that she assumed he loved her. It was too soon for that.

Sadie was not entirely sure she wanted to hear that proclamation from him. Love wasn't a word that she trusted. Those that "loved" you were often the ones that hurt you. Then again, most of her lessons on love had come from family. Some people said you should never desert your blood, but Sadie did not believe that at all. Family was nothing but an excuse in her mind. It meant that parents could treat their children however they wanted, because children should honor their parents. Sadie had refused to do that the minute she walked away from them.

Leaving her entire world behind had not been easy. At one point, she had thought that if James had gotten help and admitted what he had done, that she would forgive him. If he had given breath to the words she had needed to hear, she might have seen her mother one last time before she died. But he had not. Instead, Sadie had kept radio silence, not once telling her truth to anyone except her sister, who apparently thought it appropriate to tell her mother. Sadie could not afford to think about her mother's feelings right now. The woman was dead. All that was left was a ghost of a memory of

71

a woman who had worked her fingers to the bone to provide for her family. Sadie liked to think she would do the same for her family, if she ever had one.

Sadie heard a ding on her phone. It was Justin. *Sorry I had to go. You were sleeping so soundly.*

Sadie smiled and texted him back. *Just woke up. Thank you.*

The phone dinged again. *For?*

Everything. There were far too many things to list.

Home by 3. Be there.

Well, that answered one of her questions. He did want her to stay. But what if she wanted to leave the house? She wasn't all too sure she wanted to stay here by herself. If she did, Sadie would only have her thoughts to keep her company.

It was almost as if he read her mind. *Spare key on kitchen counter.*

Great. I'll be here.

You better be.

Sadie fought the urge to giggle. Was he always this demanding? Not that she blamed him. She had already run away once, but it wasn't him that she had been running from. Sadie had been trying to outrun the emotions that circled inside her. If she had learned anything in life, it was that the emotions always caught up to her. Sadie should have known better, but her fight or flight had kicked in and she had picked the easy way out. Running away, pushing those who tried to care for her as far away as she could, those were her greatest defense mechanisms. Today, though, she wanted to pull him closer, to learn whatever she could about herself as she let herself fall into something completely dangerous. Love? Perhaps. Could she be brave enough to experience it?

Yes. She could. She'd already walked down the other road too many times to count. It was time to break that cycle. Sadie could have something real for the first time in in her life. Well, she hoped she could. It was still too early to tell. For all she knew, Justin could just be living out his teenage fantasies. It didn't matter though. Sadie would take whatever she could get. Today was the start of a brand new day, and she would make every moment count.

Her first step? Being the best Sadie she could be. Sadie had spent forever cutting corners and scrimping where she could. Her rainy day fund was filled to the brim, but she'd never touched it. She could never afford to, that was what she'd told herself. Sadie never wanted to feel like she was living paycheck to paycheck. Her entire life had been that way, watching her mother struggle to pay the bills while her bum of a husband squirreled away a small fortune.

That was another story entirely. It was like a cloud lifted and the sun had finally come out. The doubt lingering inside her was a faint whisper, one she probably should listen to. She had an idea where this road would lead — disaster, more than likely. But Sadie wanted to live instead of merely existing. It was time to make a few changes.

She glanced down at the bland clothes she had packed in her bag — button up shirts, slacks, starchy things that helped her hide herself from the world. When she went out to the bars, she usually wore jeans and a T-shirt. That had usually been enough to attract a man to her side. She could have worn a paper bag over her face for all those men had cared. An easy screw, no complications. That had been attractive enough for them.

73

That may have worked in the past, but Justin was different. She knew she didn't have to change herself to keep his attention, but Sadie felt comfortable enough to show more of herself — whoever that woman happened to be.

"Time to make a change, Sadie girl."

She chose her clothes for the day and laid them out on the bed. Walking from the room, she looked for the closest shower. There was a bathroom right next to the guest room. Opening the closet, she pulled out a fresh set of towels and placed them on the hooks near the shower.

"Crap!"

She had forgotten her soap. Sadie quickly went back to her room to get her showering things, then returned to the bathroom. The quiet around her was almost deafening. She had never liked the silence. It made her jump at any small noise. She had to remind herself that she was safe here, that no one was going to attack her out of the blue. This fear had followed her most of her life. That was why Sadie often had some kind of background noise on whenever she was alone.

Turning on the shower, she listened to the slow roar of the water as it fell down, splashing on the tile beneath. She took a deep breath and moved back to the door. Turning the lock, she closed her eyes so hard her head started to hurt. It was always two steps forward, ten steps back. Something great had happened last night, and moments before she had been ready to move on to even better. Here she was just a few minutes later, ready to fall to pieces. Sadie had fought tooth and nail to find the coping mechanisms that would make her triggers demolish. Triggers never went away, no matter how much work she put in, no matter how many changes she had made. They were always there, like dominoes suspended in time, ready for that one thing to push the first one over and topple everything to the ground.

Shivering in the cold, she opened her eyes and looked around her. Nothing there. No demons. No memories. No one. Nothing. It was when she was most vulnerable that she was most afraid.

"Get a grip, Sadie."

She pushed the curtain aside and stepped into the shower. As the water rushed down around her, she let the tears fall down in synchronization. Clutching the wall, she curled up as close to it as she could. She was so tired of this. Tired of feeling like her entire world was crashing down around her whenever it chose to, not because anything had happened, but just at the whim of the monsters that could never be buried, no matter how long ago they had hurt her. It was not like she liked dwelling on her past—most of the time she tried to pretend it had never happened—but she had spent a lifetime on a battlefield not of her design. Its memories attacked her even to this day. Sadie had spent years in counseling, but apparently she was not as healthy and whole as she'd thought. Maybe it was time to make another appointment.

Sadie had thought there was nothing left to learn, but there was. Sadie wanted to learn how to be happy. She wanted to bask in every minute of it and not second guess the moment. For the first time in her life, she felt deserving of it. Not because she had felt amazing in his arms, but that she had finally found her voice. Sadie had faced her own personal hell yesterday, and had come out slightly bruised and banged up, but no less damaged than when she had walked into the fray. With a courage she did not know existed, she had come back to the one thing that could destroy what was left of her sanity. The fact that she was still standing told her there was a lot more to her than she had first thought. So today, she promised herself to take one step at a time, finding a deeper meaning to life besides the one that had been forced upon her. Did that mean she would not topple at the first sign of despair? No. She was human, imperfect, but fashioned from the strongest pure will any human being could have.

She wiped her eyes with her hands. "You are safe."

Yes, she was. Safe. Free. Ready.

Chapter 10

Sadie spent the rest of the day out exploring Benson. She found a few clothing outlets, where she chose some outfits that were more feminine that she was used to. Dark colors were usually her thing. Sadie had always known how to attract the wrong thing, but right now she did not need to attract a quick fix to her loneliness. She was gearing up for a fight for so much more — herself. She deserved so much more than she had allowed herself over the past eight years. So much more.

"That looks amazing on you," complimented one of the sales associates.

Sadie looked at herself in the mirror. Her dark brown hair contrasted with the pastel pink dress. She could not remember the last time she had worn pink. Sadie was so used to pushing all the girly things away from herself. Color was not something that belonged in her wardrobe. She smiled at the woman.

"I think I like it too."

"Are you new in town?" The blonde asked her curiously.

"I'm just visiting a friend."

"You look awfully familiar. Did you go to Centennial?"

Crap. Sadie did not want to be recognized. That would lead to far too many questions. "No. I don't believe so."

She lied. It was a harmless one, one she hoped didn't come back and bite her in the ass later. She just wanted to be someone else entirely, at least for one day. Besides, it wasn't like she was going to spend the rest of her life in Bensen. Sadie knew she could not live so close to her demons, and it was not like there were wedding bells ringing. She would not trust them if they were. That was much too soon, too fast. No one should ever move that quickly.

"I think I'll take it."

"Good choice. I'd recommend the yellow too." The woman pointed to the one she had tried on earlier.

"I think you're right."

Sadie gathered the two dresses in her arms, leaving the four others that had not really fit her well. As she walked to the register, she saw a few lacy undergarments, the likes of which she had never purchased for herself before. It was always whatever fit and was cheap enough not to break the bank. Seeing as most of her days were spent at work, she didn't really care what she looked like under her clothes. No one there was going to be looking at them. What would it hurt to feel a little sexy? Sexy was not a dirty word. On an impulse she bought three complete sets.

By the time she had left the store, she had spent what she considered a mini-fortune, but for the first time she didn't worry about the price. She tried to kid herself that she was buying them for herself, but really she wanted to feel the way she had when Justin looked at her last night. Beautiful.

After treating herself to lunch, followed by a manicure, Sadie returned home to get ready for Justin's return. She put on one of her new outfits, a brightly colored tunic over a pair of skin hugging leggings. Sadie knew she looked good, and best of all, she felt comfortable in her own skin. The fabric was so soft she felt like she was wrapped up in a hug. She flipped through the stations on the television in the living room, and curled up on the couch watching some made-for-TV romance. Sadie had not intended to fall asleep, but her eyes drifted shut as the sun beamed in from the windows across from her.

She was not sure at first what made her wake up. Maybe the sound of the door opening, the change of the light over her face, the sound of another person's breath, but none of those thoughts threatened her the way she'd thought they would. Opening her eyes slowly, she saw Justin standing over her, relief on his face.

"What's wrong?"

"I was afraid you'd left." He looked as if he were hiding something else.

"What happened?" she prodded further.

"Your sister came into the office."

"Oh dear lord. I'm so sorry." Sadie sat up immediately and put her head in her hands. "I'm not sure I can keep doing this, Justin."

"What?" He sat down on the couch next to her. "I'm not afraid of Katie."

"You deserve better than all this." She gestured to herself and refused to meet his eyes.

79

"You deserve better, Sadie." His words were like an anchor. "I know being here only makes it worse for you, but I want you in my life."

"I want you too. But it's...complicated."

How did she tell him she would always be looking around her to see if some ghost was still there haunting her? How could she get him to understand that anywhere that reminded her of home would be too much to bear? As much as she wanted so much more with him, she might not be able to have that when they were so close to her past. Bensen was not Taylorville, but they were so closely linked it might as well have been. If Katie knew she was here, she would be knocking on the door. Neither one of them deserved that.

"Then let's uncomplicate it. Marry me."

"*What?*" Sadie looked at him as if he had lost his mind completely. How in the hell would that uncomplicate things?

"I've loved you for half of my life, Sadie. No one has ever compared to you."

Sadie felt sick to her stomach. This should be something a woman wanted to hear, and part of her wanted to throw caution to the wind. But the sane part of her was leading her right now. She did not want Justin to throw his life away on her. He would spend the rest of his life trying to fix the damage of her childhood, and that would only make him miserable in the end.

"You can't say that."

"Why not?" He pulled her hands into his, and she was fighting every reservation she had.

"Because...people do not just get married after sleeping together."

80

"Some do. And I don't want you because of that. I mean, I do want to do that again. In fact, I've been mentally undressing you all morning."

Sadie punched him on the arm with her fist and tried to joke her way out of it. "Justin!"

"But seriously, consider it, Sadie. I love you." His green eyes were filled with more than just desire, and it was an emotion that was not one she had seen before.

What if she said yes? It would ruin everything they had just started. She knew it would. There wasn't an inch of her that wasn't aware of that. "Justin, I care a lot for you."

He let out a deflated sigh and dropped her hands. "Right."

She realized her mistake. "Justin, please. Listen to me. I am not saying no."

His eyes met hers and she saw the light start to blaze within them. "What are you saying then?"

"I need time. I want to love you. I don't know how." God, how she desperately wished she could be on the exact same page with him. To feel the warmth of someone else's love flowing deep within her veins. How easy it seemed for him, and how devastatingly complicated it really was.

"I'll teach you."

His words broke her heart in so many ways. She wanted to believe him, wanted to trust that it was possible, to know what it felt like to blindly follow him down any road. She wanted that. Sadie had never wanted anything so much in her life. Tears fell down her face as she thought about all the years she had wasted being so lost and alone. He was a lighthouse calling her in before she crashed against the shores. He might be safer if he turned the light off. Then she couldn't bring her

ELISSA DAYE

disaster into his life. How could she ask him to take all of that on?

"You deserve so much better, Justin."

"I haven't found it anywhere else, Sadie. All I want is you."

He pulled her into his arms and she laid her head on his shoulder. He stroked her hair and the tears fell down her face, ugly reminders of how broken she was inside, so broken she could not bask in the love of the man sitting before her. She really hated feeling this way. That she did not deserve happiness. How many times had she waited for it all to turn to crap? Surely that would happen sooner or later. Once he got to know her, all her flaws and insecurities, he would leave. Sadie would self-destruct and it would all fall apart, because deep down inside Sadie did not feel like she deserved to feel happy. It never lasted.

"Sadie, I'm not going anywhere." It was as if he could read her mind.

"You can't make that promise."

"I can and I do."

"Why?" She sat up so that she could see the truth in his eyes.

"Because I love you."

Sadie could not stop the words before they left her mouth. "Prove it."

Justin swept his hand through her hair and pulled her head back, gently exposing her sensitive spot where his hot mouth blew softly before it devoured her flesh with his lips. With his hands behind her back, she let her back fall against them. She felt her nipples start to grow tight as her stomach

82

clenched deliciously. If he wasn't careful, she would turn into a puddle right here on the couch.

His hands pulled at her tunic, slowly sliding it up her body before tossing it on the floor. His mouth covered hers and she lost all rational thought. She was sure that if he continued to do this for too long she would follow him down any aisle he pleased. His fingers made a path of fire down her body, every inch of her attuned to his touch. He was like the Pied Piper, playing her like the strings of a high-strung violin. Her body wept with joy, as every inch of her tingled for whatever might come next.

When his mouth started to travel down her body, she enjoyed every moment of it. She tingled and burned for so much more. His hands barely skimmed over her bra, but the instant he ran his fingertips over her nipple, she thought the tight buds were straining so hard against the garment that it would rip the lace. She loved the friction of the lace over her nipples as he rubbed his fingers back and forth.

When she moaned, his fingers pushed the lace aside and his mouth latched onto her nipple. Sadie arched into his mouth, every inch of her core now throbbing painfully inside her. It had never been like this with anyone else. He had the ability to incinerate her with just one touch. Sadie's hands went to his hair. She wove her way through his dark locks, pushing him away, yet pulling him closer. Her body was so conflicted.

His mouth continued to suckle on her as his hands moved down her body. He pushed her leggings down her legs, her underwear following. Before she knew it, she was completely exposed before him, with the light of day streaming down around her. Sadie panicked slightly and tried to sink into the couch.

Justin noticed her pulling away and sat up to look down at her. "Beautiful."

The way his eyes looked at her he could have been a hypnotist, for she believed what he said. She had never seen herself as beautiful before, but she had never seen herself through his eyes. That love in his eyes — what would happen to her heart if it withered and died? Did Sadie want to be there to find out? Someday she would do something and it would ruin everything.

"Stop that, Sadie."

"What?" She said, almost pouting from the tone of his voice.

"Stop thinking. Get out of your head. Just feel."

"I can't...."

He came down to her ear and whispered, "You can."

She closed her eyes and tried to live in the moment. His lips traveled down the length of her again, stopping just before where her legs curved together. His hands pried her apart, and he took her into his mouth. The smooth silky tongue slid along the length of her, and she almost came undone. Never had a man gone down on her like that before. Sadie was quickly learning it was one of her favorite things, as her body climbed higher and higher. Before she knew it, her hips were moving slowly as her body rose and fell against the gentle massage. The faster he stroked her, the more she wanted to push him away, but she only managed to pull him in deeper. When his finger slid into her depths, she cried aloud, "Yes!"

Something built inside her, something that was strange

and new. Like a gentle rose opening its first petals to the morning light, Sadie felt tingling start in the pit of her stomach. It grew and grew until she felt it in every inch of her body, even down to the toes that were curling painfully into the couch. She burned and ached, wanted to find out what lay just around the edge.

"Please...," she whimpered.

She felt his fingers stretch her insides to accommodate more of him. When he stroked against something on the inside of her, she felt like she was going to lose her mind. Deeper and harder his hand took her, and she was nearly breathless in anticipation—of what she did not know. The first slow quivering shook her body, but it was followed with a gut-wrenching spasm as her entire body prepared her for the orgasm of her life. Painful bliss followed as a fire filled her. She needed him to stop so she could let her body catch up to the plateau the rest of her was floating on, but Justin did not give an inch. He continued to work her over until another one followed closely after.

When he finally gave her quarter, her body was weak. She felt like she had run a marathon, but no race could ever feel as wonderful as this. Heaven help her, as tired as she was, Sadie wanted so much more. Her eyelids were so heavy, and sleep beckoned her. Sadie gave him a weak smile and tried to pull him closer. She was not used to being a solo participant. She wanted to give him just as much as he gave, but he pushed her hands away.

"Don't you want to?" Her words were hollow even to her own ears.

"God, yes. I want you more than the air I breathe." His

hand caressed her face.

"Then why not?"

"Because I can wait." He smiled at her.

"I can't...." She didn't know how to ask him. Her body craved him, and she would feel cheated if he denied her.

"Sadie...."

"Please, Justin." She had never begged anyone before, not like this. And while she should probably feel foolish doing so, Sadie did not.

Her hands went to his belt and slowly started undoing it. Sitting up, she brought her mouth up to his, not caring that his lips contained her essence. That act made him growl against her. She continued to undo his pants, the heat rising up in her again as she imagined how good it was going to feel when she pulled him into her body.

In a matter of seconds, she had helped him remove his pants. When he was exposed he looked as if he were ready to stop. Sadie ran her legs around him and pulled him closer to her. She wanted him, her body was in control. Her head would take over later. The minute he slid inside her, she felt his heat. She felt herself melt around his fire and it was amazing. Her whole existence quivered around him as he pushed deeper into her.

"Yes, oh, yes," she cried out as he pumped faster into her.

His mouth caught hers and their tongues dueled for control until their tongues seemed to match the rhythm of their bodies colliding together. Sadie wanted to live in this moment forever, but she knew it would not last. She felt the need in him as his body was taut above her. He was trying to rein himself in. Sadie didn't want him to. She wrapped her legs around him and pulled him deeper in.

He broke their kiss and groaned. "This won't last long...."

She felt the force of him pushing into her and called out his name. "Justin!"

It was all he needed to lose the rest of his control. He plunged into her faster and harder, until he spent himself deep within her. Sadie could feel his cum trickle down her leg as he kissed her shoulder. It should have freaked her out, knowing that she had not protected herself as she usually did, but Sadie already knew where her heart lay.

"Yes."

Justin's head jerked up and his eyes met hers. "Yes?"

"Yes, I'll marry you." It was the craziest thing to ever have left her lips. And while she should regret it, Sadie did not. She had very little to offer him, but he wanted her nonetheless. As she looked into his eyes, Sadie saw a joy she had never seen in any man's eyes before.

"Yes!" He shouted to an invisible audience. "She said yes!"

Sadie was shocked by his exclamation. "Are you all right?"

"Amazing. You?" He asked her cautiously.

"I'm...I dunno what I am." Sadie was being honest. She did not know what to call this feeling. It was something that had evaded her most of her life. A tear fell down her face. "I think I'm happy."

"And I plan to keep you that way."

Chapter 11

Later, as they ate their take out at the kitchen table, she saw Justin fumbling with his phone. "What are you doing?"

"Ordering us tickets to Vegas."

"What? Justin!" She shook her head at him. "You can't be serious!"

"You said yes, didn't you?"

Sadie's next words caught in her throat. She had said yes. That was not true. She had not only said yes, she had actually said she would marry him, and she had meant it. But now that time was slipping past, she started to second guess her sanity. "Justin...."

"You did say yes, right?" He looked at her as if he waited for her to say the words.

"Yes. I did say I would marry you." Sadie felt a blush fill her face. She was still not sure what had come over her. His lovemaking was intoxicating. She was pretty sure he could convince her to rob a bank if he wanted. "You didn't say when, though."

"Sooner rather than later. If I let you slip out of my sight, you might change your mind." As he contemplated that, his face grew even more obstinate. "I love you, Sadie."

"Don't you want a nice wedding?" Sadie was stalling, trying to buy herself enough time to think.

"Do you?" He asked her in all seriousness. "Would it make you happy?"

Sadie let out a loud sigh. She was fairly confident that he already knew the answer to that. Sadie did not want to be the center of attention. Putting on a white wedding dress and parading around for the rest of the world to see, that just did not sound like any kind of fairytale she wanted. "No."

"Do you want to marry me, Sadie?" His eyes probed hers.

She wanted to say no — it would be so much easier to walk away than it would to move forward. But that was a path she had traveled too many times to count. "Yes, I do."

"Will your answer be different in a few months? A year? Two years?" He challenged her.

"No. I don't think it would, but we don't really know each other." Not the way she thought they should. He knew far more about her than any man ever had. But what if he learned more later and changed his mind? She was fairly certain he knew all her skeletons. "You might change your mind."

"I won't."

"I snore."

"It's endearing," he teased her.

"I steal the covers."

"Then I'll have to hold you closer to keep me warm."

"I cry an awful lot."

"My shoulder can handle the flood." He grinned at her. "What else you got?"

"I'm cranky when I'm hungry," she warned him.

"So am I, especially when I've been starving for a long time." His eyes told her he was not talking about food.

"What if I'm not enough?" she asked him.

"What if you're more?" He reached out to touch her hand. "I know you've been hurt, Sadie. Any fool could see that."

"I've known a lot of fools...."

"I'm no saint," he countered.

Sadie giggled softly as she remembered just how much he had proved that earlier. "No, sir. You are not. But you're mine."

Justin reached across and pulled her into his lap. "Yes, ma'am. Forever, if you'll have me."

Sadie melted into his embrace, and felt for the first time that maybe everything would be okay. She didn't want anyone to save her—she'd spent enough time dumping buckets of water from her sinking ship. She'd become quite used to the fight. But maybe she could share the load. She pulled his face down to hers and sighed against his lips.

When Justin pulled away, he grinned at her. "So, Vegas?"

"Ugh...Justin! Fine, but I have a couple of things that I need to say."

"Okay. Fire away."

"I can't live here."

He looked a little hurt. "What's wrong with my house?"

"It's not the house I mind. I can't live where ghosts haunt me, Justin. I know your work is here." She didn't know what else to say. How could a relationship thrive if she was so busy fighting to keep the darkness at bay? He was her new start, but that could not start here. Not when Taylorville and all it represented was so close.

"It."

Sadie felt like it was a death sentence to their relationship. She felt the tears fluttering near her eyelashes. "I'm sorry. I don't think this can work."

"You are stronger than you know, Sadie." He put his finger on her chin and made her keep eye contact.

"I'm not strong. I've broken into so many pieces this week I don't even know how I am put together." She was honest with him.

"You're not broken, Sadie."

"Yes, I am. This whole conversation makes me want to head for the hills. I don't do love and marriage. It's not in my vocabulary." She wanted to push away from him, but her hands refused to comply.

"And here you are, letting me love you." He smiled softly. "And loving me."

"Yes...I do love you." The very admission nearly shook her to the core. "But we barely know each other."

"We've known each other all our lives."

"Yes, but how much did we *truly* know?"

"Enough to lust after each other even after all these years."

"Justin!" She admonished him. "That is *not* what happened."

"Speak for yourself. I pulled your file on purpose, I'll have you know."

Sadie shook her head in disbelief. "Are you a stalker?"

"Not that I know of. Although I've known a few." He

shuddered slightly, as if remembering something distasteful.

Sadie could see why a woman would want to get her claws in him and never let go. He was almost too perfect, from the way he handled her when she was triggered, to the way he made her feel like the most beautiful woman alive. And he was hers, right? He wanted to marry her. She never had to walk away from him. The only thing she had to do was make it work here. Could she find the strength to do that?

"I'll be with you every step of the way, Sadie."

"Except when you're at work. What am I supposed to do, Justin? I have a job somewhere else too, you know."

"One that you hate. You could quit it."

Quit? She could do that? Sadie blinked a few times. She had spent her adult life working her fingers to the bone, just trying to make her way in the world. Should she be offended that he suggested she quit her job like a bad habit?

"And what do you suggest I do?"

"Whatever you want to do. Find another job. Don't. Open your bookstore. Who knows, maybe we'll have kids."

Sadie's breath caught in her throat. "You want kids?"

"I do. Don't you?" His eyes studied her face for any kind of reaction.

Sadie lost the ability to breathe. Being a mother terrified her. What if she screwed them up? There were so many dangers in this world. How in the world could she protect them from all of them? One thought broke through the panic—the image of a cherub face with Justin's green eyes. Yes, she wanted children. She'd never known how much until that very minute. Her voice came out in a surprised whisper. *"Yes."*

"Then what are we waiting for?"

"Your family...." Sadie tried to stall, to give her brain time to think.

"My parents are gone, Sadie."

"What? When?" How had she not known that? She felt awful for not knowing.

"They're not dead, Sadie. They moved to Australia." He grinned at her.

"Australia?" She couldn't believe they had picked up and moved like that. How in the world had they been able to afford that? "Really?"

"Turns out, my father is very good at investments. They went there on their honeymoon. They love it there."

"Wow. You must miss them." Sadie smiled as she remembered his parents fondly. "Won't they want you to wait for them, Justin?"

"They already know."

"What?" Sadie looked at him as if he had lost his mind. "How could they possibly know?"

"Well, not that you said yes. I haven't told them that yet. I told them I had found the love of my life, and I was going to marry her the first chance I got."

"Oh." That one word sounded so flat. "And they know it's me?"

"They knew back then." His grin was filled with boyish charm. "At least they suspected."

"Your sister?"

"We haven't spoken in a while." The smile disappeared.

Sadie looked away and felt a sadness enter her heart. "She would probably hate this."

93

"Claire hates everything these days. That has nothing to do with you."

"I should have been there for her." Sadie sighed and leaned her head on his shoulder. "Why does everything always have to be so complicated?"

"It doesn't. You love me. I love you. We're getting hitched. Then I can have all the Sadie I want."

"Brute!" she teased him. She felt the rise and fall of his chest as he laughed under her.

"Yes, but I'm your brute."

"It would appear that you are." She sat up and pushed away from him. "What am I going to do with you, Justin?"

"Ravage me?" he suggested.

"Can we take this just a little slower?" she suggested.

"What did you have in mind?"

"Well, you've pretty much gotten me moved into your house, married, and pregnant." Pregnant...the idea was still growing on her.

"What's so wrong with that?"

She paced near the counter. "Well, there is a proper order to things."

"Order. Bah. Let's make some chaos, Sadie. We can leave in the morning. All you have to do is click this box right here." He held up his phone.

Sadie closed her eyes and tried to get her mind to focus. What was she supposed to do? What was the right thing here? She had never felt the way she did about anyone. It was dangerous. She wanted to, but she knew it was not the right thing to do. "Justin...I can't. Not like this."

"It was worth a try." He pulled her into his lap, and his

mouth captured hers in a slow heady kiss that only hinted at what would be waiting for her if she let him continue. Sadie moved away from him and left the room.

When she looked back at him, she saw he was reading something on his phone. Back to work as usual. Sadie sighed to herself. Just because she wasn't ready to race off with him and get married did not mean she didn't want him still. Sadie took that chance to remove her bra from under her shirt. She tossed it at him and tried to hold a serious look on her face when his eyebrows rose curiously.

"What are you doing, Sadie?"

"Wouldn't you like to know?"

Justin dropped his phone on the table. "Yes, I think I would."

"You seem occupied...." Sadie had already removed her leggings, and was tugging at her bottoms as if that were the next thing to go. When he did not move, she let them slide down her legs.

"And if I just sit here, you're going to.... Yep...lose it all." He whistled aloud and pushed away from the table.

Sadie barely made it out the door before Justin had caught up to her. Sadie was almost breathless when he pushed her up against the wall. Her lips were prepared for his, just as her body craved the touch of his hands. She could not get close enough to him—even if he lived inside her soul it would not be close enough. Sadie wanted to be the woman he deserved, but she knew she had a lot of work to do.

Sadie was glad that he was no longer wearing his button up shirt, for sliding her hands up his T-shirt was so much easier. Pushing it up, she waited for him to take the hint. He broke their kiss long enough to take his shirt off. His mouth moved over hers even when her hands slipped beneath the band of his pants. When her fingers made contact with the tip of his penis, he groaned against her mouth. She tried to yank them down his hips, but his erection seemed to block its path. Before she could change her method of attack, Justin took over for her.

"I've always wanted to do this," he whispered against her ear.

"What?" Sadie had no idea what he was talking about until he slid her arms around his neck.

"Hold on to me, Sadie."

She did as he asked. "Like this?"

"With your legs too...." He had the eyes of a man who was clearly up to no good, but Sadie trusted him.

As he lifted her up she wrapped her legs around him, and when she did, she was surprised to feel him slide right into her. "Oh...I see...."

With her back firmly supported against the wall, she relaxed against him as he pumped into her. He nearly took her breath away with the ferocity of his movements. She didn't mind one bit. She took every inch of him, and reveled in the wildness he stroked within her. When he came within her she smiled, imagining all the things that could happen if she just let herself believe.

"That was even better than I imagined," he said before he kissed her on the mouth. "You all right?"

Her voice sounded far away when she answered him. "Yes...good. Very good."

"Just good?" He nibbled at her neck and Sadie trembled

around him. "Oh, what you do to me, Sadie."

"Hey, this was your idea."

"You stripped first," he accused her playfully.

"I was going to take a shower," she lied.

"Like hell you were. But we could still do that." He let her legs drop from his waist and smacked her butt cheek playfully.

"We'll see about that." She scooted down the hallway, shrieking as he chased her.

Chapter 12

Monday came faster than Sadie wanted it to. It was surreal to be back at work. The tiny walls of the cubicle stared back at her with their slate gray fabric, boring, like everything else in her life for the most part. Sadie liked it that way. It was easier to maintain the existence she had come to count on. She had her small circle of friends, her work, and her apartment. It had always been enough. And yet, now she realized she was barely touching the surface of what life could be.

Sadie sighed and looked down at her phone. Was it wrong that she was dying to see the first text from him? She felt slightly pathetic when the morning dragged on and she had not heard from him. Maybe she had imagined the whole thing. The whole week was pretty outrageous, the more she thought about it. It was entirely possible she had made it up. She could have an overactive imagination.

She was prepared to keep going with that train of thought until she checked her email. Her bank had sent her a message to let her know that they had received the check from the attorney's office. It would take several business days for the check to clear. Two and a half million dollars did not move slowly, after all. Sadie's eyebrows rose in shock as it hit her. There was a lot she could do with that money, but she was loath to touch any of it. It represented a culmination of all the times they had all gone without, something she would one day come to terms with. Today was not that day. Instead, she focused on her work, and tried not to keep her phone in sight.

By the time half her morning had passed, Sadie could stand it no longer. She was about to pick up her phone to text him, when one of the office administrators interrupted her. "Ms. Turner?"

Sadie almost jumped out of her seat. She put a hand on her heart, and turned around. "Yes?"

"These came for you." Mrs. Jones handed her one of the largest bouquets she had ever seen in her life.

"Oh...thank you." Sadie did not know what else to say. Her face flushed as she stood up to take them from her.

"Looks like you have an admirer." Mrs. Jones winked at her.

"Um.... Yes, I suppose." Sadie tried to push her curiosity away.

"Was it an old flame? Didn't you go back for your father's funeral?"

"Stepfather, and yes, I had to go through the house and settle the final affairs."

There had not been a funeral that she knew of, though. If there had been, it happened long before she came to town. In fact, she didn't even know what happened to his body. She probably should have asked that, but it hadn't been something she cared to know. Truthfully, it was for the best if she never knew that information. She might be too tempted to make a fool of herself at his gravesite. Sadie had always imagined she would dance on his grave the day he died, but his death had only caused indifference.

"So?" The woman was clearly digging for more information.

"I saw an old friend. He probably sent these flowers to offer condolences."

Sadie did not want anyone else knowing her business. She kept her work and personal life separate for a reason. Well, a few reasons really. She didn't really have anything going on in her personal life. And if she did, it wasn't something she felt like sharing with people who were more strangers than anything else.

"Oh...looks like more than condolences."

"Thank you for bringing them by. I need to get back to work."

Sadie set the flowers on the corner of the desk and turned her back on the woman, hoping that she would take the hint and leave her be. Thankfully, the woman disappeared nearly as quickly as she had arrived. Only then did Sadie open the envelope that was still sealed shut. She double checked that, because she didn't want anyone else knowing her business.

Mrs. Williams One Day. The first line on the card made her roll her eyes. He sure wasn't going to let that go. It was her fault though. She had only encouraged it by saying yes. Now that she had, she couldn't just take it back. And if she were honest with herself, she didn't want to. She might not be ready to rush into a Vegas wedding after a week, but Sadie knew he would break her down eventually.

Her fingers brushed over the next lines. *I will wait forever for you.*

Sadie took a deep breath. She felt emotions near the surface, as her heart swelled unexpectedly. Tears formed in her eyes, but she would not let them fall. Words like that made her feel like having a good ugly cry. They should make her happy, but they tortured her soul in ways no one would ever understand. She put the card in her top drawer so no one would sneak a peek at what she considered extremely private. Sadie was not prepared to talk about her engagement, if it truly was one. It wasn't like she had a ring. Thank goodness. That would attract attention she didn't want, plus it might make this too real.

It was at that moment she received a ding. Sadie looked down at her phone and smiled softly.

Do you like them?

Sadie knew he must had received confirmation of their delivery. He must have been sitting at his desk watching for the very moment the flowers were checked in. She couldn't help the smile that formed on her face. The warmth in her heart, she could not deny it no matter how hard she tried. The flowers were beautiful. A bright arrangement of so many different colors.

No roses? She teased him.

You hate roses.

How did he know that? She wracked her brain over and over. Time turned back in her head, and she remembered the one time she had gotten a flower. She was a freshman in high school, and the student council was doing a fundraiser selling flowers with messages. Sadie had gotten a flower from a secret admirer, but had never known who it was. She did remember he had asked about it, and she had told him she didn't care much for roses. That if someone really loved someone, they would pick something more original.

You're too perfect, she messaged him.

I'm an overachiever.

She could almost see his face as he typed it. Was he grinning to himself? She closed her eyes and tried to focus on what she needed to do, but her head was not in her work. Less than a day apart from him, and she was having trouble keeping on track. Sadie needed to retain some kind of control over her life. Control was what kept the demons at bay.

I miss you, she texted him. She could not deny the truth.

Road trip? He teased her with his words. Sadie could not just pick up and take off. She had work to do. It was bad enough leaving it for a week. Now her pile was twice as large, and she would have to make it up as quickly as possible.

I can last five days. She refused to give in to the temptation. He did not seem as able to.

How?

Get back to work, Justin. See you Friday.

I love you, Sadie.

Bye, Justin. She put her phone down, thinking it was finally time to get back to work, but it dinged again. She rolled her eyes and picked it back up.

Say it.

Sadie fought the urge to growl at her phone. As difficult as it was to say, she knew it was the truth. She did love him, more than anyone else in her entire life. It still scared the hell out of her. *Fine. I love you too.*

Yeah, you do. This time she almost dialed his phone to give him what for, but she set her phone down and stifled the giggles that were rising to the surface. He was incorrigible, and he was all hers.

As Sadie continued her work, her mind started to turn toward the future that was just out of reach. She wanted the things he did, but she had a lot of work to do. If Sadie wanted to have any kind of a future with Justin, she could not let him be her knight in shining armor. She had to make some changes, put some time in on personal growth. Being back in Taylorville had only served as a reminder that the past was not as far behind her as she'd thought. He wanted a future with her, a family. How could she have a family if she was still so broken inside? She had been holding her pieces together the best that she could. Justin did not need to be the glue or tape holding her together. She needed to cement them back together, build a strong base so she could share the weight of any burdens that came their way.

As far as children, Sadie had gone quite some time since her last physical. She did not relish the idea of any stranger getting anywhere near her private areas, but Sadie knew it would be something she had to endure. The idea of children had not popped into her head. Now that it had, Sadie wanted to make sure that all her parts were in working order. The future he had painted, she very much wanted it. She could already have it growing inside her, considering their lack of care for most of the week.

Sadie put a hand on her stomach. What would it be like,

growing something so innocent and pure inside her? Was she ready for that? Sadie wanted to think she was. Could she be the mother a child needed? She tried not to let her mind fill with doubts. With Justin by her side, she could become anything she set her mind to. He made her feel like she could sprout wings and fly. Someday she would marry that man. She was sure he'd keep wearing her down until then.

When Sadie went to lunch she made a few phone calls, arranging an appointment with a new counselor for this Friday, and an appointment with an gynecologist for the following week. She was actually lucky to get appointments on such short notice. When she was done with those, she called her best friend to confirm their dinner date later. It wasn't often that Liz was able to get away, but she had guilted her husband into doing kid duty so that she could make sure Sadie was okay. Sadie could not wait to let everything out. Thankfully, they were just ordering Chinese at her apartment, because Sadie had a lot to tell her. Things that she didn't want anyone else to hear. Now, she just had to wait until later that night to talk to her.

Chapter 13

By the time she made it home after work, Sadie was on pins and needles. Justin had not texted her since that morning. She had almost expected him to text her more. But then again, she had practically forced radio silence by telling him to get back to work. Sadie felt like such an idiot. Did being in love with someone make you feel so completely brainless? As if the only thing you could think about was that other person? Wasn't that slightly psychotic in a way? To only think about one person throughout the rest of your day?

"Seriously! Gahhh!" She wanted to throw something. Sadie was starting to wonder if she was unhinged. Then her phone dinged and she ran to retrieve it.

Long day. Wish you were here.

She sighed audibly. *You too.*

I can make it in 4.

Sadie laughed aloud. She tried to think of a comment worthy of the situation. Yes, please! Three if you skip the

105

stoplights? She forced her logical mind to take over. They both had to work tomorrow. He could not drive here and back with only a few hours of sleep, because let's face it, they would not get much sleep. *You are not driving here tonight.*

Spoil sport.

The door bell rang and Sadie nearly jumped out of her skin. She half-expected to see him standing on the other side of the door. When she opened the door to see Liz standing there, she must have looked disappointed, for Liz stared her down. "What's up, Sadie?"

"What do you mean?" She put her phone down and tried not to look so guilty.

Liz closed the door behind her. The short haired blonde had started to carry low this past month. Liz was expecting her second child. "Well, don't hold out on me."

"Give me one sec." Sadie quickly texted Justin, as the conversation was only half-finished.

Got to go. Company.

Who?

Sadie sighed before typing a reply. *My friend Liz.*

Liz got tired of waiting for Sadie to speak and grabbed her phone. "Just a friend? Seriously? And who is Justin?"

"Williams...." Sadie tried to grab her phone back.

"And you all type in all your words? How cute! Outdated, but cute, I suppose."

"Hey, you're older than I am." Sadie stuck her tongue out at her.

"And yet, I'm the one acting my age." Liz started to text on the phone and Sadie was dying inside.

"What are you asking him?"

"Who he is…all the things you've been holding out on me." Liz teased her. When the phone dinged again, Liz's eyebrows rose and she pursed her lips together. "Oh, Ms. Sadie, you've got some 'splaining to do."

Crap. What had he texted her? Sadie felt her heart racing in her chest. "Give me my phone, Liz!"

Liz handed her phone over to her and Sadie saw their words on the screen. The blood drained out of her face. Liz had indeed introduced herself and asked who he was. His answer was what made her mortification harder to get over. He had typed two words. *Her fiancé.* The room started to spin, and Liz must have noticed the signs.

"Breathe, Sadie. Breathe, girl. Let's sit down, shall we?" Liz ushered her to her couch and offered her shoulder. "It's okay, love."

Sadie had no idea why the tears started to fall, but once they did, she could not seem to make them stop. Liz had been to hell and back with her. They were both survivors who had met in a counseling group in college. Sadie had watched Liz sprout wings and find her true love, something Sadie had always secretly wished for but never thought she deserved. It was seeing her like this, pregnant and happy, that made Sadie long for so much more.

Sadie sat up when the worst of it had passed, and wiped her nose on the tissue Liz had already pulled out for her. "Sorry."

"Hey, it's okay. So you found a hot guy and didn't bother to tell me," Liz teased.

"Brat!" Sadie sniffed at her.

"And you love me for it." Liz wrinkled her nose.

"Maybe."

"So…we'll get back to him. How was the rest of it?" Liz knew that Sadie had gone back to confront her demons. She had practically begged Sadie to take her with her because she had known what it was like to go back.

Sadie blinked. How did she describe it? The first thing she thought of was her confrontation with her sister. "Well, I saw my sister."

"Ah, fuck. How'd that go?"

"How do you think?" Sadie sighed and took a deep breath. "She pretty much blamed me for everything that has ever gone wrong in her life."

"You didn't hand her the drugs," Liz offered.

"No, but apparently because my stepfather liked me better, it made her life miserable."

"Excuse me?" Liz made fists in her lap.

"I know. As if trading places with me would have really made her life better. I may not be a drug addict, but my life is a shit factory all on its own."

"Well, some things are good apparently."

Sadie glared at her. Liz held up a hand. "Okay, so you're not there yet. So the bitch blamed you for her life. What did she want from you?"

"The two and a half million my stepfather left me," Sadie answered matter-of-factly.

Liz whistled. "Wow…that's something."

"I tried to turn it away." Sadie held up her hands. "I don't want his blood money."

"Why not? It's not doing him any good any more. Besides, it's not enough, really. You deserve ten times that for what he did to you."

"I'm not a prostitute." Sadie threw up her hands.

"Whoa! It's not a payment for services rendered. Services are offered, not taken. You are not a prostitute." Liz looked as if she were trying to find the right words. "It's restitution."

"That's what Justin said." Sadie looked down at her hands.

"Ah...okay. So now, tell me where he fits into all of this. But first, can we order some food." She looked a little apologetic. "Blame this one. Hungry all the time. I swear, I don't know how I've only gained ten pounds so far."

"Fine. I'll order it." Sadie pulled out her laptop and looked through the menu, choosing the things that the two of them normally ordered. She checked out and closed the laptop to find Liz was still looking at her curiously.

"Is he the one, Sadie?"

"Which one?" Sadie deflected the question slightly.

"The one you've been in love with since you were a kid?"

"What? No...." Sadie could not meet her eyes. "And that was just a crush."

"You're deflecting. I remember you telling me his name was Justin. Williams?"

Damn her memory. "Yes. It's him, but it's not like that."

"Then what is it like? Look, I've got all night, and my two-year-old is being a jerk today. I'm not in a hurry to get back home." Liz wrinkled her nose. "Time for Tim to have a turn. See how he likes the turd ball."

"Turd ball?" Sadie crossed her arms and shook her head at her friend.

"What? He makes little balls out of his poop. I'm tired

of cleaning them up. I freaking hate potty training. It's like a form of medieval torture. It would be easier to let him poop on the floor. I'm just saying."

Sadie burst out laughing. She laughed so hard she thought she might wet herself. Was this what she had to look forward to? Cleaning up poop from random places? While it might sound like hell to some people, Sadie was looking forward to it. As frustrated as her friend might be, Sadie knew there was nothing she would not do for her kid. They were wired the same, the two of them. "Oh, just imagining you cleaning that up."

"You're welcome to come help."

"Not a chance."

"So...*Justin?*"

"God, where do I start? He knows...."

"Knows?" Liz stared at her for a minute before one of her eyebrows rose. "Oh...*knows*. Wow, how did that go?"

"He wanted to kill him." Sadie smiled.

"He's already dead though, right?"

"I told him that. Seemed to deflate his ego a bit."

Liz nodded. "I can see that. Knight in shining armor complex?"

"Yeah, just like Tim."

"Oh, I like him already then." Liz yawned. "Sorry, go on."

"He was with me when I went home." Sadie did not know what else to say.

"You went to the house? Why in the hell did you do that?" Liz chided her. "Sadie, you don't have to revisit your personal hell. No one has to do that."

"Well, I have to sell it. So I thought I needed to at least see what shape it was in. Don't worry, I'm fine."

"FINE?" Liz crossed her arms. "Which one? Fucked up, right? That always hits first."

"No, I mean I'm good." She was good, wasn't she? "And I'm not going back again. Not after this time. I still don't understand how he took it so well."

"What?"

"Well, I took a knife to the chair, and then I—"

"Hold on, you did what now?"

"Obliterated it. Ripped the fabric to shreds."

"And he just watched you stab a chair to death?"

"Yeah. Crazy right?"

"And what did he do after? Call for help?"

"Held me."

Liz smiled. "Good man. He's a keeper. It takes a strong man to walk through hell with the woman he loves. Then what happened?"

"I ran."

"Yep. I've done that a few times too. Good thing Tim is patient. I think after the fifth time he threatened to install a GPS tracker on me. I really have put that man through hell." Liz grinned. "But wait till he cleans up the first poop tonight. I'll have to put a tracker on him. Jacob's been eating a lot of broccoli lately."

"Oh, dear God. Should we send in reinforcements?"

"No. That man is going to take it like a champ, and then rub my feet when I get home." She grinned.

"I wasn't running from him, not really. I was running from...."

"Yourself?" Liz answered knowingly.

111

"Yes. But, I ran back, and…. Well, things happened."

"What kind of things?" Now, Liz was thoroughly enjoying herself. "Sex things?"

"Maybe."

"Hallelujah! Sadie got laid!"

"I've had sex before."

"Not the good kind. By the blush on your face, it was the really good kind."

"One thing led to another, and he proposed to me." Sadie did not know how to explain it.

"Sounds to me like you weren't the only one with a crush."

"How did you know?"

"Have you ever watched the Hallmark Channel? I've seen every fluffy romance ever written. It's on twenty-four seven. Trust me, when you're nursing a baby at two o'clock in the morning, you've seen every sappy thing ever written."

"I'm not sure about any of this, Liz."

"Do you love him?"

"Not enough to fly to Vegas and get married." She looked down at the ground.

"Well, that would be bat shit crazy. Did he expect you to do that?"

"He wanted me to, but I don't think either one of us would have really gone through with it." Sadie sighed. "I did say yes, though. Not to Vegas, but to marriage. I do want to marry him, but I want to be better."

"If you're looking for happily ever after, it's there. It may not be packaged as nicely as a fairy tale, but it does exist. So, what is your plan?"

"First, counseling. I don't want him to feel like he has to

fix me. That's my job. I have work to do still. Especially if I want...."

"What? What do you want, Sadie?" Liz was really staring her down right now.

"Kids," she whispered.

"YOU? Really? He must be really special."

"I didn't think I lived in a world where that was possible before." Her eyes misted over slightly. "Am I stupid?"

"Stupid? For falling in love? Never. That's the bravest thing you've ever done. I'm proud of you." Liz was a little teary-eyed too. "So...since you're the only one getting some, you planning on sharing some of the details?"

"You get some." Sadie tried to ward off her curiosity.

"I *got* some. Plenty of some. Now, he couldn't touch me with a ten-foot pole. Not for lack of trying, I might add. Poor guy."

"And you left him home, with poop too."

"I probably should offer a hand job at the very least," Liz added.

"Perhaps." Sadie giggled. "Oh, God. Now I'm picturing that. Let's not talk about sex for the rest of the night, okay?"

"Fine, spoil sport. Won't even let me live vicariously through you."

"Through me? What a reversal."

"Don't worry so much, Sadie. It will all work out. I have faith enough for both of us."

Sadie wished she had the faith inside herself. As they settled into the rest of their night, they watched one of the adult movies that Liz could not watch in front of her kid. A comfortable silence fell over them. When Liz was almost

113

ready to fall asleep, Sadie had to push her out the door. She knew that Tim would worry way too much if Liz did not come home, and waking a fairly pregnant woman with grouchy tendencies was not something she wanted to do. She much preferred feeding her and sending her home.

Before Sadie went to sleep she pulled her phone out, reading over all the texts from the day. She sighed and went to put her phone down when it dinged at her. Looking down at the screen, she almost laughed aloud.

Did I get her blessing?

Yes. But she threatened to make you watch her kid first. Sadie waited for his reply. Liz had not threatened that, but it was funny regardless.

I could use the practice.

Of course he could. Could he be any more perfect? Surely there had to be a catch somewhere. How could she possibly have found someone like him? How had she missed the signs so many years ago? Because she hadn't dared to dream, and because her best friend would not have liked it at all.

Crap. Claire. There was no getting around it. Sometime soon, she would have to face her. With the way Justin was going, she probably already knew. What was she going to say to her? They hadn't spoken in quite some time. Time had a way of changing people. Sometimes for the better, and sometimes for the worse.

I love you.

The only words that mattered. Sadie smiled. If she could get through walking through her worst nightmare, she could get through facing Claire. "Just one foot in front of the other, Sadie."

114

Before she second guessed it, she texted him back. *I love you too. Good night.*

Chapter 14

Sadie sat in the waiting room, staring at the white walls around her, so medical and uniform. She was not looking forward to this appointment, even though it had allowed her to take a half-day at work. This was the day she would have to bare her soul all over again. Telling and retelling trauma only opened up barely healed scars, digging down to the disease that would never be removed from her body. She tried not to feel hopeless. That was not the way to start her first session with Dr. Reddick, the doctor who had taken over her last therapist's practice when Dr. Cramer had retired.

She hated the waiting. Sadie could almost hear the pass of time as her heart beat loudly in her ears. As much as she dreaded this, she knew it was important. Sadie could no longer ignore the fact that she was not nearly as healthy and whole as she'd thought she was.

The door opened and an older woman peered out. "Sadie?"

Sadie gulped and tried to clear her throat. "Yes."

"Come on in." She ushered her into her office.

Sadie willed her feet to move. She could do this. When she walked in the door, Sadie almost breathed a sigh of relief. The room was not the stale white color of the lobby. Instead, it was a pale blue that was peaceful. She looked around the room and found different pastel landscapes that were much different that what she remembered in this office before. There was a dark blue rug on the floor with pastels woven into it. Sadie could lose herself in the print easily. That was her habit. Losing herself in the little things, while she delved into the topics that were too hard for her to deal with on her own.

"So, Sadie. Dr. Cramer left me her patient files when she left the practice, but I did not see yours there."

"It's been a few years." More like five, but Sadie did not want to say that aloud.

"So what brings you here?" Dr. Reddick sat down in one of the large arm chairs and gestured to the comfy couch before her.

Sadie sat down and pulled the pillow into her lap. She started to squeeze the tips of the pillow before she could get any words out. "I hate this part."

"I know, dear. I know, but I can't help you if I don't know where to start."

Sadie looked down at the carpet and followed one of the pink swirls with her eyes as she spoke the first words. "I'm a survivor. My stepfather sexually abused me up until the day I left."

"How old were you when it started?" Dr. Reddick had a notepad in her hands, but her eyes were trained on Sadie

117

instead of what she had written down.

"I'm not sure. Five? Seven? Depends on what you mean." There were many different scenarios that popped into her head, none that she particularly cared to speak about. "I was eighteen when I left."

"Sounds like a lifetime," Dr. Reddick interjected.

"It was. Sometimes it felt like eternity." A tear fell down her face. "Sorry. I just don't like to think about it."

"Tears are healthy, Sadie."

"They don't feel healthy."

"How do they feel?" asked the doctor.

"Dangerous." That was the only word to describe how it felt to feel so emotional. "We were never allowed to cry. Never allowed to be angry. Never allowed to...."

"Feel?"

"The only thing I felt was fear. When I was little I was told if I didn't stop crying he would give me something to cry about."

"Sadie, look at me."

Sadie did not want to look at her, but she did. "Sorry, I'm just very emotional. I went home last week to deal with his death. Just seeing that house again...."

"You went back?" Dr. Reddick was impressed.

"Yeah. I went back."

"Wow. That's—"

"Stupid?" Sadie interrupted her.

"Brave." Dr. Reddick smiled at her. "Incredibly brave."

"It was the hardest thing I've ever done."

"Do you know how many people never go back? If it was easy anyone could do it. It takes a strength that is undeniable."

118

"I wasn't alone. Justin was with me."

And he was with her now, as she talked, in her heart, almost as if he stood behind her as she poured out her soul to the woman in front of her. Sadie continued to tell the counselor about everything that had happened during that week, leaving out specific details that would make her too embarrassed to come back. The doctor did not need to know about the sex, only that it had made her feel. She went on about how much she wanted to have a future, and how that wasn't something she had ever dreamed of before.

By the end of the session, Sadie was feeling drained, but Dr. Reddick had given her a few exercises to try at home. The first thing was journaling her feelings, writing down any time she felt an attack coming on, or when she felt like running. Sadie knew that she could not continue to run from her feelings. If she ran from Justin too much more, she could lose him in the end. Right now, she wanted to give them both a fighting chance.

By the time she left the office, Sadie knew she had done the right thing. She felt like a weight had lifted from her chest, that there was going to be a light at the end of the tunnel. Her reward? Ice cream date. She dialed Liz and waited for her to pick up.

"Hello?"

"Want to get some ice cream?"

"Hello? *Pregnant*? Remember?"

Sadie could almost hear Liz rolling her eyes on the other side. "How long will it take you to pack everything up?"

"Next to nothing, really. Grandma's on duty today."

"Woohoo! Our favorite place?"

"Ten minutes. Wait, make that fifteen. I have to add five extra minutes for the shoes."

"Got it. See you in fifteen."

Sadie drove to Carlie's and pre-ordered her friend's latest cravings. She had learned long ago not to keep a pregnant woman waiting for her ice cream. When she retrieved the bowls, Sadie carried them over to the open table by the window. She saw Liz pulling in and waved at her.

Liz waddled through the door and gave her an appreciative smile when she saw the ice cream already on the table. "Chocolate pistachio?"

"Of course."

"Oh, yeah!" Liz sat down slowly and pulled the first spoonful in her mouth. "Oh-my-god! I might have an orgasm…mmmmm."

"Liz!" Sadie chided her. She looked around the store to make sure no one else had heard her.

"What? It's a compliment to their product." She winked at Sadie. "So, how did it go?"

"It was…."

"Hell?"

"You know it."

"That first one's a bitch. It always is," Liz recollected not too fondly.

"It's like pulling a Band-aid off. It's done. Now, I can move on."

"Yes, you can. Speaking of moving on, how's the stud?" Liz asked her.

"I'll find out later." Sadie felt her heart leap in her chest. She was really looking forward to seeing Justin tonight. He was driving to her place as soon as he was finished with work.

"Oooh…someone's getting laid."

Sadie turned purple. "Liz!"

"Hey, it's the first time I get to tease you. You never reacted before."

That was true. Sadie had always talked to Liz about her booty calls. None of them had been embarrassing in the slightest. It was not like Sadie was a virgin, but the way she felt about Justin was hard to explain. He was the one. Her heart knew it, her mind was coming around to it, but she still needed time to heal. Sadie could not expect him to be the answer to her everything.

"I know. I'm all out of sorts, Liz. I don't know what's wrong with me."

"You're in love. Head over heels." Liz put her hand on hers. "I'm happy for you. And you better wait until I don't have to waddle down the aisle to get married."

"Oh, I dunno about that. I'm not into big weddings." Sadie pushed the question as far away as she could. The very idea of walking down an aisle with everyone staring at her, putting her on the spot, she just didn't see how that would ever work for her.

"No…no…no. Don't say that. Girl, I've been waiting forever to stand up with you. You have to have a wedding.'

"Why? I don't have anyone—"

"Bullshit! You got me," she chided her. "I know I can be a pain in the ass, but you're kinda stuck with me."

"I do, but I don't want to be the center of attention. All those eyes on me…."

"Oh, honey. Come on now. The only one who matters is

121

the only face you'll be looking at. The way a groom looks at his bride when he first sees her walking down the aisle, it's priceless. You don't want to miss that. It's a gift unlike any other." Her eyes got a little misty. "Oh, there you go. Now you're making me cry."

Sadie rolled her eyes. "Hormones?"

"They suck donkey balls," sniffed Liz as she gulped another bite of ice cream.

"Apparently."

"Oh, just you wait. You'll fall to pieces at anything." Liz wiped her eyes. "But that's not the worst of it. One day your boobs will no longer be your own. They're more like udders. Swollen, painful udders."

"Still trying to wean him, are you?"

"I'm down to twice a day, thank goodness."

"By the time you're done with that the next one will—"

"Shut it! Shut your mouth right now, Sadie Turner! I can maim you with this...." Liz looked down at the utensil in her hand. "Spork? What the hell are they doing with sporks here? They do realize that ice cream doesn't require ice picks, right?"

"Well, maybe someone might want a brownie with their ice cream?" Sadie pointed to the dessert bar.

"Crap! Why didn't you get me some of those?" Now Liz looked at her ice cream like it had the plague.

"I'll go get some."

Sadie decided humoring her would probably be the best bet, or Liz would probably melt onto the floor like the ice cream in her bowl. And Sadie thought she was having a bad day. She didn't mind though. Liz was her rock; maybe rounder these days than most, but still strong enough to help her slay any demons that haunted her. Sadie would forever be thankful that she had Liz in her life. The sisterhood they shared could never be replicated.

"Thank you! That looks amazing!"

"You're welcome. Thank you for helping lift my spirits."

"Of course! You know I'm always here for you." Liz smiled at her. "I'm so happy for you, Sadie."

"What if it doesn't work out?"

"Then you still get a chance to experience love while it lasts, and that is something that you never hoped for at all."

"But what if I end up broken?"

"You pick up the pieces and keep moving forward. Personally, I think you worry too much."

"Probably."

Worry had been her oldest companion though. It was familiar. Best friends with pain and misery, worry was constant. It never changed. Everything else did. Sadie wasn't sure she was strong enough to exist in a world where she might actually contemplate being happy, but she was sure going to try.

Chapter 15

Sadie was sitting on the couch in her small living room, counting the seconds as they ticked by. Not entirely certain when Justin would be there, she was in limbo as she waited for him. She wasn't sure how comfortable he would be in the small studio apartment compared to his house, but she was thankful she did not have to make the trip to Benson today. If he got off work at four, she probably would not see him before ten. At the same time, it would have been nice to know when he left.

When it was near seven, Sadie was about to text him. She was trying not to be that girl who seemed needy, but she was starting to worry about him. Well, that was not completely true. Sadie was also afraid he might have changed his mind. It had been a week since they had seen each other. Maybe he had come to his senses. Could she blame him? Sadie was more than he bargained for, she was sure of that.

The doorbell rang and Sadie nearly jumped out of her

seat. She fought the urge to race to the door. Walking as slowly as she could convince her body to go, her heart raced in her chest. She flung the door open faster than she intended, but she could not help herself. Ignoring the bag of food in his hands, Sadie wrapped her arms around his neck and kissed him.

Justin seemed to have no problem with it. In fact, he walked her backwards into her apartment, closed the door behind them, and dropped the bag of food on the floor. When they finally came up for air, he stroked her cheek with his thumb. "I missed you too."

Sadie closed her eyes as he caressed her cheek. When his mouth came down to hers again, she sighed against him. "I love you."

"I love you too, Sadie."

She was so lost in the moment, she did not notice the tears streaming down her face until Justin pulled away from her. His eyes were full of concern as he wiped them away.

"Are you okay?"

"What?" She blinked in confusion before realizing he was talking about the tears. "Oh...yes. I...."

"What's wrong?"

"You're too good to be true." It was the only words that computed with the way she felt right now. He was too perfect. The way she felt inside was something she had never felt before. Light, free, and completely terrified that it would end in a matter of seconds.

"I'm only human, Sadie. I'm not perfect."

"You're perfect for me," Sadie admitted. She had never felt like any man fit her like Justin did. None of them had made her heart feel so full it was ready to explode. None of them made her body tingle from top to bottom. Just remembering the last time they were together intimately still brought a blush to her face. She tried to clear her mind from that, because she didn't want to jump his bones the minute he walked in the door. What kind of precedent would that set?

"If you don't stop undressing me with your eyes, your food will get cold," he teased her. "You are hungry, aren't you?"

"Definitely." But it wasn't food that she craved. She bit the bottom of her lip and closed her eyes, trying to shut out the desire that was like fire in her blood.

"To hell with it."

He left the food where it had fallen on the floor and pulled her tight against his chest. His lips crushed hers in a kiss that told her he wanted to devour every inch of her.

Sadie started to undo the buttons on his shirt. When she felt his hot skin against her fingertips, she ran her nails lightly against his chest. She wanted to feel his heat against her body so badly, she was frozen in time without it.

Justin wrapped his fingers in her hair and pulled her head gently back to expose the curve of her neck. When she moaned aloud, he nibbled her flesh and Sadie thought she would crumple at his feet. Just a few caresses of his lips and she lost all reason. Justin steadied her with his hands and continued his work.

"Maybe we should...oh...mmm...."

"Bedroom?" asked Justin.

"Right upstairs." She took his hand and led him upstairs to the loft-like bedroom. When she got to the top of the steps, she started to unbutton her own shirt.

"Slow, Sadie. I want to memorize every inch." His eyes watched her like a man who was hungry for more.

Sadie was still not used to having his eyes on her, but the desire in his eyes only reassured her that he liked what he saw. She slid one arm out of the shirt, then the other. Sadie was wearing a lacy red bra that let her skin poke through at just the right places. Clearly Justin was a fan of the red, as he looked at her breasts appreciatively, making her happy with her purchase. Sadie let her hand fall down the valley of her breasts as she made her way to the buttons of her jeans.

Justin looked as if he wanted his hands to take over, but he kept himself under control. Sadie paused and waited to see what he would do. His voice came out guttural. "Keep going, Sadie."

Sadie pulled the zipper down slowly and slid her hand inside the band to slide them down. When the red panties were revealed, she heard another intake of breath. Her eyes met his as she kicked the jeans to the side. She started to move toward him, but he held up his hands.

"Stay."

"You don't want...?" Sadie was a little confused. He had the looks of a man who was ready to devour every inch of her, but he was keeping her at arm's length. She leaned back against the wall and almost crossed her arms over her body.

"Don't hide, Sadie." His words were a whisper that traveled across the divide. "You're beautiful."

"Then what are you doing over there?"

"Memorizing every centimeter." His eyes were filled with desire. "Do you trust me, Sadie?"

"Yes," she whispered.

"Touch yourself."

"Where?"

His eyes looked down to her chest and back to her face. She felt a little awkward, but the love and desire in his eyes gave her courage to continue. Remembering how he had reacted to her hand over her skin, Sadie let her hand brush over her breasts. She imagined her hands were his and closed her eyes. When she opened them, Justin looked almost dangerous. "Like that?"

"Yes. Now, move them down."

"Down...." Sadie felt the heat of his eyes trailing a path that her hands followed. She squeezed them against her flesh, the way she wanted him to do. When she slid them under the waistband of her panties, she closed her eyes and bit her lip. "Like this?"

"Yes...god, yes." His breath came out in a loud hiss.

Before she knew it, he had crossed the distance and scooped her up in his arms. Sadie shrieked. "I thought you wanted me to...."

"That's about all I can take of that right now. My turn."

Justin lowered her to the bed and his mouth and hands took over. Sadie sighed as his hands moved over one of the lacy cups. His thumb stroked over her nipple and she whimpered slightly. Oh, how she had missed this. Every inch of her was already aching for him. He moved the lace down and his mouth devoured her breasts, licking her areola, which was now becoming rigid against his tongue. When he sucked her nipple into her mouth, Sadie thought she would lose her mind. She arched against him and her breath caught in her chest. She did not breathe until he released it. Her break was only short-lived, because he repeated the process with her other breast.

By the time he released it, she was nearly ready to scratch a path down his back—the desire was already hitting a feverous pitch. Sadie did not know how much more she could take, and she realized he had just gotten started. He trailed kisses down her stomach, alternating them between nibbles. Everywhere he touched, a mad trail of fire followed. His hands moved her bottom all the way down her legs, and his lips seemed to follow. It was as if his mouth were memorizing every inch of her flesh.

When he came back up her leg, she felt his hands push her legs apart and she closed her eyes, waiting for him to finally penetrate her, but he did not. Instead, she felt the warmth of his tongue as he caressed the folds of flesh. She was far past aroused—she was about to lose every inch of her sanity. His hands squeezed the cheeks of her butt as he pulled his face in closer. Sadie could not help but topple over the edge as his mouth took every inch of her in. Hot desire worked its way through her body, making her feel dangerous as she moved against his face, riding the wave he was creating so deliberately.

When he finally pulled away, every inch of her was throbbing. He paused only to remove his own clothing. Sadie watched every movement, cataloging his flesh into her brain like a tattoo she would never forget. She shivered against his heat, not because she was cold, but because she wanted his flesh to cover hers. He did not disappoint. He took her mouth in his, and at the same time slid into her. Her moan was trapped in the cavity of his mouth, as he seemed to swallow her whole. Their tongues battled together as he pumped in and out of her so slowly she thought she would die waiting for him to pick up the pace. Her climax built teasingly, ever so close but so far away, as he refused to rush through it.

When the first delicious ripple twitched inside her, she felt him stiffen above her. Justin pulled his mouth away and his nose brushed against hers. "Not yet, Sadie."

"What?" She whispered.

"No finishing for you."

She lay there, stalled on the edge of the oblivion her body craved more than air itself, yet she tried to still the madness ebbing through her. Sadie whimpered when he moved slowly again, and she tried to grab onto any piece of him, but Justin held her hands tightly behind her head.

"Stay."

Sadie nibbled on the bottom of her lip and pouted at him. "What are you...? Oh...are you trying to kill me?"

Her insides clenched around him and he withdrew from her. He was clearly just as tortured as her. "Ah-ah. None of that. I want this to last, Sadie."

She looked into his eyes and realized he was tormenting himself too. That knowledge gave her ammunition. She would play his game, but in the end she would get him to break his rules. When he slid into her finally, she closed her eyes and just let herself feel every movement. The way he stroked the inside, filling her up more than any man ever could. The silky smoothness of each thrust was debilitating, as her body drank in every inch of him. Every slow movement brought a flutter of appreciation from the sheath that wrapped around him.

130

Any time she got close, she clenched around him, squeezing everything she could to maintain some kind of control. In doing so, she was driving Justin crazy.

He moved faster, and she was trying her best to follow along with his rules, but the faster he moved, the harder it was to get her mind to take over. Finally, she threw caution to the wind and let her body have its way. Like an itch burning to be scratched, it rippled slowly, growing speed as Justin continued to push into her. The more he moved, the harder it was to fight as her inside exploded, sending waves of pleasure through her entire body. She shook against him, not caring that she had broken his rule. Her core squeezed him in tighter as she bucked against him.

She knew Justin could not pull away even if he wanted to. He was so caught up in her orgasm as he rode it harder and faster, that her flesh rippling over him sent him over the edge. She felt him cum inside her, and almost lost her mind as another orgasm ripped through her. Sadie wanted every inch of him, refusing to slow down her pace just because he had gotten his. She wanted more, and it was his fault for building the frenzy within her. He stayed hard long enough for her to get herself off one more time, before he collapsed on top of her.

She did not mind his weight. Her body accommodated it. Sadie felt him still planted firmly inside her as his cock seemed to twitch. It was as if his body and mind had two different ideas. He was as exhausted as she was, but his body wanted more. The thought of him getting hard so fast made her throb even more. When she thought there might be a round two, he pulled out of her and pulled her into his arms.

He kissed her forehead. "God, I missed you."

Sadie sighed. "Me too."

Sadie felt a sleep coma beckoning her, the kind only good sex could create. Her eyelids fluttered open and shut. She had not intended to fall asleep, but she had not slept well over the past few days. Justin must have sensed her need, for he pulled the covers over them and pulled her into the curve of his body.

Chapter 16

The next morning, Sadie awoke to smells coming from the kitchen. Her stomach rumbled angrily, and she realized she had not eaten dinner the night before. She got up to use the restroom and make herself a little more presentable. When she was done, she picked up Justin's shirt from the night before. She buttoned it up over herself and let herself smell his scent. Ahh. If she could just bottle that up and keep it with her always.

When she made her way into the kitchen, she found Justin standing at her stove making what smelled like an omelet. She walked over to him and slid her arms around him.

"That smells delicious."

He turned around and kissed her on the mouth. "Good morning."

Yes, it was. Any day she woke up with a gorgeous man making her breakfast was better than any other morning. She smiled up at him as he checked out her choice of clothing.

"I think it looks better on you."

Sadie could tell he was already trying to figure out how to get her out of it too, but she was too hungry to play into it. "Bacon?"

"Yep." He held a slice up for her.

Sadie nibbled it hungrily. He must have gone out to get it, because she was fairly certain she did not have bacon anywhere in her house. "That's divine."

"I've made you some coffee too."

Was there anything he wasn't good at? How in the world had no one seen this handsome man and snatched him up? Sadie was a very lucky woman, something he drove home every time she saw him. He had already changed her life in so many ways. She could not help but wonder what the future had for them. She wanted to give him everything he deserved. The more they had talked about children, the more she realized how important they were to him. While he had his sister, Justin had always wanted more siblings. His dream was three or four kids. Sadie would be good with two, maybe three. There was a part of her that longed to be carrying one already, no matter how impetuous that may sound.

"Thank you." She kissed him on the cheek and went to make a cup for herself. She sat down and watched him as he continued to make breakfast, wondering what she was supposed to do with her time at the moment.

When he set the plate down on the table before her, her eyes met his. "You're so good to me."

"You deserve every bit, Sadie."

Did she? He seemed to give so much to her and take very little in return. She took a bite and let his words hang before them. She had no idea what to say to that. "Delicious. Is there anything you can't do?"

"Convince you to move in with me." His eyes met hers.

Sadie felt her heart leap into her chest. She wasn't ready to do that, was she? After one week away from him she felt like she'd lost a part of herself, but Sadie wasn't sure that was enough to make her pick up and leave everything she had created by herself.

"Think about it, Sadie."

"I have a life here."

"But you live more when you're with me." His eyes were filled with concern. He was worried about her.

Sadie did not want to feel so far so fast. It wasn't fair for him to come into her life and disrupt the order she had fought so hard to maintain. But he was right—she was miserable without him, but that was a misery she had to face right now. Sadie had just started to work on the things that would make a difference for both their lives. She wanted to be healthier, to be able to mentally support herself so he did not have to feel responsible for every drop of her happiness. "Don't worry so much, Justin. I'm okay. Better than okay."

"Oh?" He asked her curiously.

"I started counseling." She threw it out there, afraid he would worry more hearing that she was seeing a professional. Everyone had their own opinion about therapy.

"For?"

"I don't want you to feel like you have to fix me all the time, Justin." The words were out before she could second guess them.

"I'm not fixing you," he countered.

135

"That's not what I meant." Sadie sighed. She was not trying to upset him. "I just don't want my past to hold me back."

"From?"

"Happiness. You make me happier than I've ever been, but…."

"But?" He looked worried.

"I'm afraid I'm going to lose it all." Sadie looked away. This was not the conversation she had intended to have today. Her insecurities were always getting in the way. Damn them.

"Hey, look at me."

Sadie's eyes met his, and while she was tempted to dash the tears away from her eyes, she let him see the raw emotion on her face. "I've never wanted anything more in my life than you."

"Why so sad then?"

"I'm not…damn it. I'm happy." She wanted to throw something at his smiling face. Damn him. This was not funny. Sadie had spent a lifetime fighting the urge to cry, and here she was a blubbery mess. What was wrong with her?

He reached for her hand. "I will wait as long as it takes, but you don't have to be alone."

"I'll keep that in mind."

"They have counselors near Benson too," he pointed out.

A logical suggestion. Sadie would consider it. "I just wanted you to know I was taking steps."

"As long as they don't take you further away from me, I'll support any step you make."

"Thank you, Justin," she whispered.

"For?"

"Being you, being patient, kind...amazing."

"Sexy? Desirable? Insatiable?" he grinned at her.

She rolled her eyes and started to eat the rest of her food. "And a decent cook."

"Damn skippy. I know how to keep my woman happy."

He did. Sadie didn't understand how it all came so easy to him. It was almost like he'd been in a relationship with someone just as needy as her before, but from what he'd told her most of his relationships were casual, much like her own. She tried not to think about it too much. The past had already screwed up most of her life. It was time to stop dwelling on it so much.

"So, what would you like to do today?"

Many things came to mind, and all of them required them staying home, but Sadie knew they needed to do more as a couple than just having sex. They were still relearning each other from the years of their youth.

"Movie?" he suggested.

"It's been a while since I've been to one of those," Sadie answered.

"Movie it is then, followed by...." He definitely had the same thoughts she did.

Now that Sadie was done eating her food, she returned the plate to the sink. She was about to walk around him when he pulled her into his lap.

"Where do you think you're going?"

Her eyes met his as she caught the breath that was stuck in her throat. She could feel his erection through his pajamas, and it made her tremble inside. "Didn't you get enough?"

"Have you met me?" He teased her. "I could never get

enough of you, Sadie."

He sure knew what to say to a girl. As his fingers started to unbutton the shirt, he slid his hand inside. It rubbed against her nipple that was already hard, and he groaned. As he pushed the shirt away, it was then that he realized that she was not wearing anything under the shirt at all. "This is now my favorite shirt."

"Why's that?"

"Because every time I wear it, I'll be thinking about you naked beneath it."

His mouth captured hers and he let his hands move down to her behind. When he massaged it gently, she moved against the erection that was teasing her through the cloth. He moved his hands briefly, and when she brought herself down against him, this time he slid into her.

Her breath caught in her throat and she bit her bottom lip. "If you keep that up, I might have to move my timeline up."

"My plan all along." He used his hands to help her rise and fall.

Sadie leaned over as she rode the length of him, letting her nipples tease his flesh. His fingers squeezed her cheeks almost painfully. Sadie clenched him as hard as she could, and he drove into her faster. She could not focus on anything but the way he pushed her closer to the edge. Riding him like the stallion he was, she let the frenzy carry her, taking him in and pushing out as she continued to work him over. It was hard to tell who was mastering who by the time she collapsed into his arms.

He held her tight against him and stroked her back. Sadie could not help wishing she could stay forever just like this, in the strength of his arms and the love of his embrace. She wanted eternity more than anything. Her fear was the only thing that held her back. It was something she would have to conquer if she was ever going to move forward.

"So...are we still going to a movie?" he asked her.

"Sure," she answered him.

"Popcorn?"

"Extra butter, and Milk Duds."

He chuckled. "Of course. But we don't want to forget the Twizzlers."

As his erection pulsed inside her, she realized he was definitely ready for round two. "Oh...that's not a Twizzler."

"I should hope not."

"Sure does have a mind of its own," she teased him as he moved into her slowly.

"I like where it's leading." He caught her bottom lip in his teeth as she brushed hands across his nipples.

"I can't comp...oh...that's nice." She felt herself dripping around him, and wondered when her faucet would turn off. She had never been this wet in her life. He seemed to be the only man who could turn her on switch on and keep it turned up until she had no will to resist any inch of him.

When the chair started to creak underneath them, Justin stood up, still firmly planted inside of her. He cleared the table with one fell swoop, and Sadie heard objects crashing to the floor. Sadie gripped the sides of the table as he continued to push into her. He brought her legs around him and she pulled him in closer.

"Uhmm...you feel so good. So wet. God, I can't get enough of you."

Sadie clenched. She loved the sound of his voice, raspy and raw, when he was overwhelmed with desire for her. Her ass hit the table over and over as he rode her harder. Sadie arched her back and waited for the orgasm that threatened to erase her sanity. "Oh, God, yes!"

Every inch of her quivered around him and he lost his mind over her. He rammed into her so hard she could hear the table shaking underneath her.

"Yes, oh, yes," she called out.

She wanted, needed, what she could not vocalize. She had no idea where else he could possibly take her than he already had, but the fever climbed so high she thought she might evaporate before him. Sadie did not realize there was an even higher plateau to climb, but when the orgasm hit her it was so violent and raw that she almost shied away from it, but the force of it nearly took her breath away. Sadie had not even realized Justin had finished too. She heard him calling her name, but it was like he was a million miles away. The world was hazy around her, as if she were trapped in another world that was hidden to the rest of the existence.

"Sadie?" His voice finally broke through.

"Hmmm?"

"Are you all right?" He seemed concerned.

"Mmmm...." Was her only response.

"I'll take that as a yes," he chuckled, and pulled her up into his arms.

Her whole body was numb and tingly. She felt like he had given her the good drugs. They should bottle this feeling up and market it to the rest of the world. Love was definitely the best drug. She snuggled her head against his shoulder as he carried her upstairs.

"Where are we going?"

"To sleep, I think."

Her eyelids fluttered opened and closed. She tried to push his hands away. "What about the movie?"

She never heard his answer, for the minute he curled up in the bed beside her, Sadie fell into a blissful sleep.

Chapter 17

The weekend went much too fast for Sadie's liking. They did eventually make it to a movie, where they shared a smorgasbord of treats. The future was not long from their conversations as they talked more about what they wanted out of life. Sadie was starting to picture happiness near in the future for the first time in her life.

She was excited to see him tonight. Sadie was making the drive to see him after she finished her appointment at the gynecologist. She had quite a few questions for the doctor, especially since she had not seen one for several years. Sadie knew she should have been going every year, but the truth of the matter was she didn't care for some stranger poking and prodding down in that general vicinity. It was not a pleasant experience for any woman, especially someone who had been through a traumatic experience.

Sadie stared at the door, feeling more exposed than ever in the paper gown that barely wrapped around her ass. How in the world would this cover a pregnant woman, let alone any woman who was larger in size? Standard sizing simply did not apply to every woman. Too bad the medical world had not caught up to that fact yet. Or were these gowns being made in a country where the women were categorically smaller?

Her heart jumped in her chest when the knock sounded on the door. "Ms. Turner?"

"Yeah…," her voice almost squeaked.

The door opened and a tiny blonde walked in the room. "I'm Dr. Trent."

Thank God! Sadie was hoping they had put her with one of the female doctors. She had asked for whoever was available, although she had hinted that she was a survivor of childhood abuse, so maybe they had planned ahead? She did not know what to say to the doctor. Nice to meet you? Sadie was beyond nervous. She had changed her underwear twice before she finally made it there, not because she had an accident, but because she wanted to make sure she wasn't being judged by the state of her underwear. Because doctors expected fresh and clean, right? she teased herself. She knew it was the nerves making her crazy.

The doctor looked over her chart. "Looks like it's been a while. Some questions we like to ask, especially with your history. Are you in a relationship?"

"Yes." Sadie did not know what that had to do with it.

"Do you feel safe?"

"Yes."

"If you are not in a safe situation, it's my job to let you know you can speak up at any time. We're all trained here to get you the services needed to find a safer place."

Wow, really? Sadie was actually surprised to hear that. "No, I'm good. In fact, I'm engaged."

"Congratulations!"

"I…uhm…I have a few questions." Sadie nibbled her lip.

"Fire away."

"Well, one really. I would like to have kids. I just never thought it might happen. I have irregularly painful periods. I think…well…I was abused at a young age."

"Yes, I see that. I'm sorry to hear that. Have you talked with someone?"

"Yes. I'm in counseling. I just kinda wondered, could that stop me?" Sadie was terrified of what the doctor would say.

"Well, I'll be able to answer that after I examine you, but to really know we would have to do extensive tests. Let's just start with an exam."

Sadie laid back and shut her eyes. In the past she would already be freaking out, but she latched on to the hope she had walked in here with and refused to waver. Please, please let it be possible. Please, she whispered over and over in her head. She tried to ignore the tight pinch of the speculum, but she had never had a pleasant encounter with of those cold metal beasts.

"Almost done. I'd recommend some blood work too. When was your last cycle?"

"I'm due for one next week." Well, she would be if she was on time. Sometimes she was off a week. Part of her hoped that was the case, because it might not just be her cycle going crazy. She could be pregnant even now. They certainly had not protected against that.

144

Dr. Trent had a serious look on her face. "I did feel some scarring, Sadie."

"What does that mean?" She didn't want to breathe in case she missed the doctor's answer.

"I'm not sure yet. But it can impede the process."

"Can I get pregnant?" Sadie's worries fluttered to the surface.

"We would have to do more tests to investigate further. From what I feel, it's not enough to make an exact diagnosis. But there is a chance that the scarring could be problematic in conception."

"I might not be able to have kids?" Sadie closed her eyes and tried to not imagine the worst-case scenario.

"I'm so sorry." Dr. Trent pulled her gloves off and put a comforting hand on her arm. "That's not exactly true. Would it be as easy as someone who did not have the scarring? No. Is there risk? That I can't say until we get a better look."

Tears fell down her face as the doctor helped her up. Sadie became a messy puddle of tears. "It's not fair. He's still ruining my life, no matter how far I lift myself up."

Dr. Trent's eyes were filled with compassion. "If it's in my power to make it happen for you, I will. I won't give up on you, Sadie."

Sadie's lip wobbled pitifully. "So there might be hope."

"Never give up on hope, Sadie. Look at how far you've come," the doctor pointed out. Not that Dr. Trent had one iota of a clue of the distance she had traveled in her life.

"Okay." She wiped her eyes with the tissue the doctor handed her.

"Okay. I'd like to order some blood tests after your next

cycle. If you have a little longer, I can do a pelvic ultrasound. Then we can determine if a laparoscopy might give us the answers we need."

"Okay."

"Okay. Sit tight, I'll be right back."

When the doctor returned, she had a small portable ultrasound. She held up a small rod. "This is what I use to do a transvaginal ultra sound. It can be slightly uncomfortable. I insert it inside so I get a more accurate picture."

"Okay." Sadie appreciated her explaining what she was doing before she did it. It helped her prepare for the awkwardness of the moment. She lay back, and while she usually would be freaking out about anything probing inside her, she was more focused on the fact that she might not be able to have children. Please let it be wrong…please be okay. Sadie did not want to hear her next words.

"Yes. There seems to be scarring, but I'm worried there might be more there that I'm not able to see. What's your schedule like? I really would like to get a closer look. I know I have some availability in the next couple of weeks."

"I'll make it work," Sadie answered without thinking. "If you find more, what can we do?"

"We can try to resolve the scarring. Try not to think about it, Sadie. We'll figure something out. Let's wait on the bloodwork until after your next cycle. That can be a good indicator of how strong your hormone levels are." The doctor removed the wand. "Do you have any questions for me?"

"No." Her answer sounded hopeless even to her own ears.

"Try not to worry, Sadie. You're just beginning the process

here. We've got options." She offered a few more encouraging words before leaving the room.

Sadie closed her eyes as the door closed. She tried to remind herself it was not the end, that this door had barely been opened, but that didn't mean it was already closing. The biggest fear in the back of her mind was, what if she was not enough for Justin? He wanted a family. She knew there were other options, but would he want to tie himself down to someone who couldn't give him what he wanted? He had given her all of him; maybe he had taken them down this road too fast. Sadie had a lot of imperfections that he not only tolerated, but accepted without question. This one imperfection was the one that might break the scales, though.

Sadie pulled on her clothes, feeling numb for the first time in weeks. She was familiar with this void. How was she going to make her way to his house and pretend everything was okay? Did she tell him what was going on? Would it chase him away? Sadie just could not face that right now. She resolved to pretend that everything was okay. It wasn't like she had definitive answers yet anyway.

Sadie fought the urge to call Liz right now, because she knew Liz would know even by the tone of her voice that something was wrong. And forget texting. She was like a blood hound. She would figure out her predicament with any strand of words she used, so even that form of communication would not work. Sadie took a deep breath and left the room. She told the desk assistant to tell her when the next available time slot would be so that she could have the laparoscopy done.

When she got to her car, she saw she had missed a message

from Justin.

Can't wait to see you.

As sad as she felt, just seeing his message made her feel a little better. Her steady, loving Justin. If he could continue to love her through it all, Sadie would make it. With him, anything could be possible.

On my way, she answered him. Sadie sighed as she put the phone on the car charger. What she needed was a little distraction. She turned on the loudest, upbeat music she could find, hoping it would keep her mood at bay. Like anything else in her life, this was just another mountain she had to climb. She prayed the climb was not rocky, covered in mudslides, or avalanches. She liked her mountains steady, like a rock. Easy to rely on and resolute.

Chapter 18

Sadie did not even have to walk up to the door. The moment she pulled into the drive, Justin was already opening the door. She smiled when he made his way down the steps. She barely made it out of her car before he pulled her close to him. She sighed against him when he wrapped his arms around her.

"Rough day?" he asked her.

"Just female stuff," she answered him.

"Oh?"

"Our physicals are a little more excruciating." She wrinkled her nose at him and kissed him on the cheek.

"My poor sweet baby. Want me to yell at the doctor?"

"It might help, but only a momentary fix," she giggled. Besides, Dr. Trent was actually trying to help her. Not that she wanted to explain that to him. There would be time for that, time to burst the bubble she was hiding inside with him.

"Everything all right?" he asked her.

It was the perfect opening, but Sadie could not bring herself to destroy the illusion of happiness that was surrounding them. She wanted to stay in the moment a little longer and ignore the dark stormy clouds in the distance for as long as she could. "I'm a little tender."

"We'll take it easy tonight then. Light cuddling. Let me get your bags. Did you bring something fancy?" he asked her.

"Yes." It had been an odd request, but she'd brought a dinner gown that she had found during the week. She had no idea what he had planned for the weekend, as he had not been too specific about where they were going tomorrow. Sadie was just going with the flow.

When they went inside, Sadie sat down on the couch. He took her bags up to his room while she sat there thinking about everything she was trying to avoid. The what ifs crept up slowly, but by the time he came back down she had plastered a smile on her face, the same one that had gotten her through most of her life. Sadie had perfected the art of deflection a long time ago, had become an actress to hide the secrets that had absorbed every part of her existence.

They spent the night snuggling together on the couch as they watched one movie or another. Sadie had trouble staying in the moment with the shadows looming over her. Thankfully, Justin didn't notice her melancholy. Sadie was so stuck in her head she could not climb out. Taking the news of her possible infertility would have been much easier if she did not have to consider anyone else, but she was not the only one in the equation. Their love was too new and fragile. Sadie was not sure it could withstand something like this. She might not survive his disappointment.

The next morning, she sat across from him and tried to think of what to say. She chose the first escape that came to mind. "So, what are we doing today?"

"Tonight, there is a gala we're going to attend, hence the dinner gown. It's about an hour away from here. Social event of the season."

"Oh?" Sadie tried to act like the very idea did not put her on display like the horrific spectacle she felt she was.

"It's important. Rubbing elbows with other attorneys gives me options." He could tell she was not thrilled with the idea.

"What kind of options?" Sadie was a little intrigued.

"The ability to move to another location." He looked at her pointedly.

He was trying to find a way to give them a life further away from where it all began. It should have made her love him more, but instead it made her incredibly guilty. Justin loved his house. He was proud of it. His life here that he had created, it was important to him, and he was willing to throw it all away, all to have a life with her. The guilt ate at her, an impossible feeling of doom continuing to weigh on her. It was the way it worked. Any time there was something good in her life, she always waited for the hammer to fall. This time it was a ticking time bomb that was just a few steps from implosion. Usually the excuse was something the other person had done, some quirk that she just could not handle. Not this time. Instead, it was Sadie and all her imperfections that she knew one day would ruin the man he was.

"Well, I shall endeavor to be your ravishing arm candy, I suppose." She winked at him. She would put on a gown and

151

pretend everything was all right. Maybe it would be good practice.

"Today, I thought we could visit Claire."

Claire? Wow, were they approaching that part of their relationship? Sadie felt her stomach turn flip flops. How much did she know? Would she be upset or supportive? He was just piling it all on top at once, wasn't he? Today would be one of the hardest days of her life. She felt like she was about to walk on blazing hot coals. Would her fragile ego be able to take the fire, or would she burn up under its flames?

"Okay. So, Claire, then your gala." Sadie felt like she was being tested to see how well she could fit with the rest of his puzzle pieces. Was he measuring her? Or was she doing that to herself? Either way, she felt like she was under a microscope, and the day had not even started.

"More pancakes?" he offered her.

Sadie was actually not that hungry. In fact, the thought of food today made her feel slightly nauseous, but that was to be expected with the amount of stress she was under. It took everything she had not to race to the bathroom right now, but Sadie held it together. "I'm good, thanks."

"You barely ate. You all right?"

"I'm fine." And today she meant it. She was fucked up, insecure, neurotic, and emotional all at once, even if it was hidden far beneath the surface. But he did not have to know that. There was no sense in ruining the day he seemed to be looking forward to. "When are we leaving?"

"As soon as you're ready."

She stood up and started to clear the dishes. Standing over the sink, she sighed when he put his arms around her belly and kissed her neck. What she wouldn't give to just stay in his arms forever this way, supported by the love that blossomed between them. This was when life slipped away and all that was left was the beauty that passed between them. She loved him with all her heart, more than anyone in her entire life, and she prayed that would be enough to get through the struggles that were about to come. She felt them hovering, like the Grimm Reaper waiting to take its new victim. This time it was not going to be a person, but the only thing that had been right in her life.

His hand caressed her belly. "One day you'll be barefoot and pregnant in this kitchen."

The ax fell and the moment was lost. Sadie closed her eyes and tried to will the tears not to fall. It was one of the only times her body seemed to listen. She fixed a smile on her face and turned around to kiss Justin on the mouth in the only deflection she had left.

When his hand brought her close, she felt strength in his embrace. It was almost enough to chase the clouds away. As his hands moved under her shirt, Sadie giggled. "Do we have time for that?"

"There is *always* time for that." He kissed her until her last doubt left her head, and every inch of her was now on notice.

"Well then...." Sadie pushed out of his embrace and headed out of the kitchen.

"Where are you going?"

"To bed, Mr. Williams."

"Is that an invitation?" He asked her, but she never answered.

Sadie walked up the stairs, attempting to still the beat of

her racing heart. Even with the storms ahead, she could still have this moment before the rain fell down around them. All she had to do was stay in the moment. The moment she made it to his room, she stripped down and climbed on top of the bed, striking a pose that she knew would only entice him.

When he entered and saw her lying across the bed suggestively, he took his clothes off and tossed them on the floor. Sadie watched him as his beautiful body crept across the floor. She was memorizing every inch, cataloguing it in the back of her mind. She wanted so much more than a lifetime, eternity, but she was afraid to tie him to a future that would make him unhappy in the end.

Closing her eyes, as his body pushed down on the bed, she sighed when he pulled her back against him. Skin to skin, his heat to her shivering cold. His mouth trailed kisses down her back and Sadie sighed against him. When his hands roamed up her stomach, her muscles bunched up in reflex. They continued to move up until they brushed against her nipples. Sadie arched against him and sighed.

His lovemaking was gentle, as if he were taking great care with every move he made. She fought the urge to pull away from him and retreat from the love he gave to her, knowing deep down inside she had already decided it was coming to an end. She wanted the frenzy, the crazy wild love that they had before. That would be easier to walk away from, but the tender caring man who was above her would be much harder to lose. Every inch of her wanted more of him, but she could not let herself hope for much more than the few moments they had left.

When it was over, she sighed against him and tried to

throw the shutters up before he could see the fragility she was trying to hide. Whether he noticed her torment or not, he never said. Instead, he gathered her in his arms and stroked her back softly with his hands. She knew he was probably imagining the life they were going to have as they lay there together in that moment. All the while, she was already dreading its destruction.

Chapter 19

The drive to the sober house was longer than Sadie thought it would be, mostly because her whole world was moving in slow motion. She could not make it speed up no matter how hard she tried. Her life was fading before her eyes. She kept a smile plastered on her face, hoping to keep it hidden from the rest of the world.

"Cat got your tongue?" Justin asked her.

"Oh, sorry. Just tired, I guess." She faked a yawn and stretched her arms. It was partially true though. Sadie was tired, more so than usual, but she knew it was stress eating at her.

"We'll make this as quick as possible," he promised.

"That's what you said earlier," she teased him.

"It's not my fault you're so irresistible."

"Likely story." She rolled her eyes, then took a breath and reminded herself that miracles could happen every day. When he smiled at her, she believed almost anything was

156

possible. She pushed the clouds away to the furthest corner of her mind. Her insecurities would have to wait.

As they pulled into the parking lot, Sadie took a deep breath. "I'm nervous."

"Don't be."

"Have you told her about us?" Sadie should have asked him before now, but she had been distracted by one thing or another. Now that the moment was here, she was almost terrified of what her friend would have to say to her after all these years.

"Yes."

"And?" Sadie almost died waiting to hear his reply.

"She's being Claire."

What did that mean, "Being Claire?" Did that mean she did not approve? Sadie sighed as she tried to count to ten, a technique she'd employed a long time ago. She had not used it in quite some time. Her mind was already filled to the brim with other worries. She did not need this one too.

"Don't worry, Sadie." He lifted her hand to his mouth and kissed it. "The only opinion that matters is mine."

So, there were opinions. Not good ones apparently, or he would share them with her. Now she felt like she was walking into the lion's den. She tried to prepare for whatever came, but she was already feeling ready to run before they even walked in the door. Her eyes met his, and she knew she would walk through fire for that gaze.

They made their way into the rehab house, and found Claire waiting for them on the back patio. Sadie was surprised at how thin Claire had become. She had never been overweight, but now she was extremely thin and underweight. Her blonde hair was tied behind her head, but the bright luster Sadie remembered was gone. Claire gave her brother a smile, and Sadie saw the cracks and stains on her teeth, the eroding remnants of years of drug abuse.

"Claire." He leaned over and gave her a hug.

Sadie stood there, unsure of what she should do. She crossed her hands in front of her to hide from the hardened stare that Claire threw her way. "Claire, it's good to see you."

Claire nodded to her. "And you."

Why did Sadie feel like that was far from the truth? She sat down across from her, wondering what she should say to someone she had not seen in so long. Their relationship had always been so easy, but here and now, Sadie did not know if it even existed. The cool glance was all Claire offered her. "How are you doing?"

"I've had better days. Today is not one of those."

"Oh...." Sadie looked down at her hands.

"So, you came back home?"

"Yeah, well, just for a little bit."

"It's a bitch, isn't it?" Claire's words surprised her.

"What is?"

"Going home."

"Yes, it is." Thank God. It was like a lifeline had been tossed to her.

"Nothing's ever the same when you leave." Claire looked as if she were lamenting that at the moment.

Sadie did not have the same sentimentality. "That's not always a bad thing."

Claire looked as if she wanted to say more. "So, congratulations are in order, I suppose? Why don't you go get us some *mock* drinks so we can celebrate, Justin? That will give us a few minutes to catch up."

"If you're sure?" Justin looked over at Sadie to make sure she was okay.

She wasn't, but this was going to happen whether she wanted it to or not. It would probably be better if he weren't here to witness it. "I'm fine."

Again with the word that she had never defined for him. It was the one real thing that would have told him how not fine she really was. He nodded at her before leaving the room.

"All right, let's hear it."

"Smart girl. Look, Sadie, you know I love you."

All the worst things started with "I love you." Most of them anyway. She knew this was not the good kind. "But?"

"I love my brother more."

"And I'm no good for him?"

"He told me about your issues."

"Issues?" Most of the hairs stood up on the back of her neck. "So, I'm the dirty little secret you don't want attached to your family?"

Claire's eyes filled with sympathy. "No, that's not it at all. I'm so sorry you had to go through all that. If I could change what happened to you, I would. God, in a heartbeat. No one deserves that."

"There's a but in there." She felt tears gather in her eyes. Deep down inside she had always known the truth. She was not good enough for him, and Claire had seen it immediately.

"My brother deserves better."

"Right." Sadie closed her eyes and waited for the rest to come. It never ended with just that.

159

"He's spent half his adult life taking care of me, Sadie. Seeing me in and out of rehab. I'm a lot to handle. He's given up so much to be here for me."

"I see. So what you're saying is—"

"That he doesn't need another project, another person to save. He seems to be attracted to one tragedy after another. Like Jenna."

"Jenna?"

"His college girlfriend had an eating disorder. He tried to save her life, but in the end she went a little crazy."

"Oh." So she was not the first person he had met who had needed a knight in shining armor. That did not surprise Sadie. He was pretty good at being selfless.

"All he wants is a normal life with a wife and children. He almost had that before with Nikki."

Another name he'd never mentioned. He had told her about the college romance, but not about the one that followed. Sadie did not say a word, as she was processing what Claire was telling her. In a matter of minutes, she understood more about Justin than she ever had. Was it even love he felt for her? Or the need to rescue another person? Was that his disease? Everyone seemed to have one.

"She aborted their child," Claire threw in.

"And he wanted it?"

"Yes. Of course he did. Justin loves kids."

Sadie felt crushed inside. Maybe that was why he wanted children before. The woman he had loved had taken the chance to be a father away from him. It was a wound that probably still hurt. And here she was, probably barren for all she knew. How could she take that dream away from him

160

too? "So, it all comes down to me not being good enough for him?"

"He needs someone to love, not a project." Claire's words were not said to hurt her, but Sadie was crushed nonetheless.

"Claire! That's enough." Justin's voice was so quiet it was near deadly. He set the glasses down on the table.

"Justin, you deserve —"

"To love who I please. You don't get to make that choice for me. If you can't accept that, then maybe you should rethink your place in my life." He was having trouble maintaining his composure. "I think we'll be going now."

Sadie was still looking down at the floor, hearing Claire's words ricochet in her head. They were the same words she had been trying to keep at bay. He did deserve better. When he offered her his hand, Sadie took it. As they walked away, her eyes met Claire's and she nodded to her, as if to tell her that her words had been heard. Their exchange was invisible to Justin, who refused to turn back to look at his sister.

"Wait, Justin. Just wait a minute."

He stopped in his tracks and turned to look at her. "She's wrong, Sadie."

"She's your sister. She loves you," she admonished him. "You need to make peace."

"If she can't accept you —"

"Justin, if you don't go over there and make sure she knows you are not going anywhere, we will be here a really long time." Sadie already knew that their relationship was doomed. She did not want to be responsible for putting a wall between the two siblings who clearly cared for each other. They always had.

He touched her cheek before kissing her softly. "Only if you promise to forget everything she said to you."

She gave him a weak smile. "Already forgotten."

He leaned over to her ear and whispered, "*Liar.*"

Yes, that was her. A big, fat, ugly liar. She was holding secrets she should tell him, but she couldn't expose them. Not today. Tomorrow — well, tomorrow was going to be another day. "I'll wait in the lobby for you."

Sadie left him and went in search of a soft chair to collapse upon. She closed her eyes and begged herself to make it through just one last night. If she could lay in his arms one last time, maybe it would be enough to last her entire life. God, she hoped so. If she prolonged the inevitable, she might never find her way out of the fog again.

As she sat there, she had a lonely fantasy in her head. The image of a child reaching for her face with its tiny pudgy little fingers, with eyes as big her father's, a small little girl with a smile that brought only rainbows and unicorns. The best parts of her, a dream for the innocence, hidden behind her lids. The small gurgling laughter that bubbled to the surface when the wonders of the world were revealed to her one at a time. The image was the most breathtaking thing she had ever imagined, because she had never dared to dream about the possibilities.

She opened her eyes and reality came crashing in around her. To know that she might never have that experience broke her into so many pieces that she knew she would never be able to put them back together. She could not allow that same destruction to take over his life too. Sadie closed her eyes and took a deep breath. It was time to close her heart, to push her longing away.

Chapter 20

They were quiet for the car ride home, which suited Sadie just fine. She wasn't sure she wanted to get into it with him. The moment the car stopped in his drive, the silence was finally broken.

"Sadie, we need to talk."

"Rip the Band-aid off?" She smiled sadly.

"She shouldn't have said what she did."

Sadie got out of the car and closed it softly behind her. She walked to the house, trying to think what she should say to that. Nothing seemed safe at the moment. As she entered the house, he was right behind her.

"Sadie, you have to let me in."

But she had. Too far, too fast. She had known better all along. Sadie was not meant for this life. She let out a sigh. "Very well, Justin. Say what you need to say."

"What does that mean?"

"That you need to talk about it. I just want to forget it."

Sadie started to pace back and forth in the room, waiting to hear what would happen next.

"I made a mistake."

His words broke her stride midway. Sadie's breath was an audible gasp. She had not expected him to say that. Turning to face him, tears were already falling down her face. "Yes."

"I should not have taken you there," he added with his hands up defensively.

That was not the mistake he had made. Just one to add to the pile, but the biggest one was making her fall in love with him. Why the hell did he have to do that to her? All the bitterness she felt inside was hard to keep at bay. "She has a right to feel the way she does, Justin."

"Her feelings are not mine. Sadie, sit down. You don't look well."

Sadie laughed hysterically as she stood there. "I don't look well? That's a riot."

He walked over to her and put his hands on her shoulders. "Sadie!"

She snapped out of it and looked at him with eyes filled with anguish. "I don't want to be your project, Justin."

"You're not a project."

"I don't want to be something you have to continually fix."

"You're not."

"Bullshit," she gritted out. Her feelings were swirling around in a dangerous funnel inside her, and she clung onto the anger to help keep the misery at bay.

"I love you, Sadie."

"Tell me about Jenna."

165

His eyes became clouded and he stepped back from her. "I haven't thought about her in a long time, Sadie."

"Do I remind you of her? The one you couldn't fix? So you have to fix me?" Sadie accused him.

"You're nothing like her."

Why did that feel like an accusation? "Right. Got it."

He looked even more frustrated at her as she walked up the stairs. She did not know what she was doing at that point, but he followed her up the stairs. Sadie tried to ignore his presence as she went into the room and started to gather her things.

"Where are you going, Sadie?"

"One of us has to have some sense."

"But you aren't making any sense," he accused her softly.

"But that's what you get with me, Justin. The best I'm ever going to be is fine, and that is not good enough. You deserve better than that." She flinched when his hand touched her arm.

He removed his hand and sat down on the bed. "Why does everyone keep deciding what I deserve? When did it become everyone else's choice?"

Sadie was nearly shaking at that point. The build up was killing her. Her body craved consolation, but she was afraid to seek it. She would never be able to turn away if she did. "Look at us, Justin. We're set to self-destruct."

"Then get your finger off the button, Sadie."

Yes, because it was all her fault. He was right. She was destroying the most beautiful thing she had, but she could not seem to help herself. "Why did you do it, Justin?"

"What?" he asked her in confusion.

"Why did you make me love you?" Her voice was almost void of emotion.

He was up off the bed before she could say anything else. "Say it again, Sadie."

"I love you?" she whispered.

"That is all that matters to me." He wiped her tears away with his thumb and put his forehead against hers.

But it was not going to be enough. Not when he found out that life with her would not be the picture-perfect world he craved. Denying him the one thing he needed would kill them both slowly. She knew she was leaving, but she wanted a piece of him tattooed on her brain before she left.

She put her hands on his face and brought his mouth down to hers. Closing her eyes, she felt the velvet smoothness, latched onto it, holding onto the feeling for as long as she could, letting it replace some of the darkness that shadowed her memories. She took the initiative for once as she started to unbutton his shirt.

"Sadie, we should talk."

"Talk is overrated," she answered him as her mouth trailed down his neck. She could sense his reluctance, but Sadie would not be dissuaded. She ran her hand down his chest and pushed the shirt away as if it were distasteful.

She undressed every inch of him and led him over to the bed. The tenderness in his eyes was mixed with a darkness that Sadie understood. She wanted him, more than she wanted life itself. Standing next to the bed, she took her time undressing before him. His eyes traveled the length of her, and she wondered if he knew this was the last time he would gaze upon her flesh, for his eyes lingered longer than necessary.

167

When Sadie came to the bed, she sat up and trailed her hands down his body, followed directly with her mouth. Every sense was engaged as she listened to the intake of his breath as she tasted his skin. She took her time everywhere she touched, trying to make a lifetime of memories in that moment.

Tears formed in her eyes and trailed down her face when her eyes met his. Justin pulled her down and kissed her softly on her lips, before moving her so that she was under him. There was a battle brewing between them. It was as if she were saying goodbye and he was begging her to stay. With every touch, every kiss, every soul-searching gaze, their bodies spoke to each other in ways their words could not communicate.

Justin tried to master the dialogue, showing her the ecstasy that came with every movement. Sadie was drawn to the rhythm like a moth to a flame. Her wings fluttered too close to the edge, and she burned up in the flames that he stoked inside her. What was fragile could not survive the cavernous differences between them, no matter how desperate she was for it to live and breathe.

When it was over, Sadie was sobbing uncontrollably. He held her as tightly as his arms could hold her.

"This is not goodbye, Sadie." His voice tried to order her to stay.

"It has to be, Justin. You have to let me go." She hated herself for saying it. She didn't want him to let her go. Every part of her wanted him to fight for her, but there was only so much strength, so much will.

"I can't." His eyes pleaded with her, as if to ask her not to go, but Sadie could not give in to them.

"This won't work. I think I've known it all along," she lied. He did not need to know that though. What she was doing was a saving grace for him. He would hate her for a while maybe. Then he would go on with his life, and the next time he might choose someone with fewer flaws, a woman who could give him the family he deserved.

"It *is* working." He refused to give in to her.

Sadie pushed away from the safety of his arms. She was going to have to learn to live in a world where his love did not exist. It had existed so easily before he came along, if that could really be considered existence. As she sat on the edge of the bed, his arms came around her. She bit back sobs and her lips shook.

"I can't give you what you need, Justin."

"I have everything I need, Sadie."

"I can't...."

He seemed to realize that forcing the issue at the moment was not going to change the direction. "If you run away, I'm not coming to find you."

"I know." She was counting on that as she pulled on her clothes. Sometimes doing the right thing for someone else involved giving up everything she ever wanted. Everything her heart desired was sitting on the bed behind her, and she was terrified to look at him. She turned to the sound of his voice.

"I love you."

"I know," she answered him. She saw the misery on his face, the tears that were near the corners of his eyes. What she was doing would hurt him, probably for longer than she cared to think about, but her mind latched on to what Claire had said. He deserved so much more than she could give him. It was as if Claire had detected the weak link in her armor, and held it up for Sadie to see.

Chapter 21

Sadie wasn't sure how she made it home without having an accident. Her vision was constantly blinded by the tears that refused to stop falling. She had stopped fighting the misery as it continued to creep through her. By the time she reached home, she had almost managed to latch onto the only friend she'd ever truly known, the blissful void of emotion she continued to hide within, hoping that no one could find her.

She stayed there for days, not really bothering to get up from her spot. All she wanted to do was fade away there, reliving her last moments with him over and over in her mind. If she could just hold onto his face before she ripped his heart from his chest. Sadie had never hurt anyone like that before. It was just more proof of the damage she did to anything in her path. She would forever blame herself for bringing all of that into his life. If she had only stopped it before it even started. But then, she would have no memories to carry with her, and even with the pain she was in, she knew someday she would be able to rise above it and see that time for the beauty it brought to her life. From here though, she resolved to be with herself until it no longer hurt to think of him, even if that took forever.

When her boss called her to find why she wasn't at work, she tenured her resignation. Sadie no longer had the will to exist in the real world with other people. With enough money to live off of for a while, Sadie knew she was going to be okay. She just had to get through this. The problem was, she didn't know if that was even possible.

His texts had come—she'd known they would. He was lost, hurt, alone. He missed her, he wanted her to come home to him. Sadie wished that she could, but eventually she knew he would come to resent her. She already resented herself enough for both of them, she knew it would come.

He had promised he would not chase her, and so far he had kept that promise. The fact that she had not answered his texts should have been proof to him that he should keep his distance. Sadie did not want him crawling down this rabbit hole with her. It was cramped and dark, covered in cobwebs and mildew. It was a place that no one should dwell. Sadie knew it well. Like an old friend, it wrapped around her and comforted her with its familiarity.

Weeks passed, and Sadie was barely responding to anything in her life. She ate, only what she could manage to keep down. Nothing seemed appetizing to her anymore. She ached in places that she could not describe, in ways she was sure she deserved. She put off seeing Liz, because she knew her friend would just see through her. Sadie came up with one excuse after the other. She caught a cold, the flu, had a headache. Some of that was true, but Sadie was having trouble keeping Liz at bay.

A loud knock sounded on her door, followed by a screeching voice. "Damn it, Sadie. If you don't let me in, I'm going to let my water break on your doorstep."

"You wish!" accused Sadie.

"Yes, that would be bliss, but that's besides the point. Open the door."

She didn't want to, but she knew that Liz was a woman of her word. She'd probably go into labor just to get her to open the door. Pushing away from the couch, Sadie fought the dizziness that seemed to swarm around her when she walked these days. Unlocking the door, she slowly opened it and glared at Liz. "What?"

"Holy fuck. What happened to you?" Liz ushered herself inside her apartment and looked around. "When was the last time you ate?"

"Ate?" she repeated like a mynah bird.

"Sit down. You look worse than I do."

Sadie blinked and tried to decipher what Liz was saying. She sat down and hugged one of the pillows to her body. As she brought it to her face, she smelled the remnants of Justin's cologne. She was half-tempted to stick it in a bag and seal it up for anytime she wanted to remember how he smelled.

"What did you do, Sadie?"

"Why are you accusing me?"

"Because from what I can tell you had the perfect man. What did you do?"

"Why do I have to be the reason it blew up?"

173

Liz's eyebrow rose. "You do realize who you're talking to, right? Queen of destruction."

"You're in good company, then." Sadie's eyes teared up, to her surprise. She had thought they would be completely drained by now.

"What happened?"

"He wants kids," she whispered through her sniffles.

"So do you."

"I might not be able to have them." Sadie looked away from her, unable to meet the concern on her face.

"What are you talking about, Sadie?"

"My appointment," Sadie sniffled. "It did not go so well."

"What happened?"

"I'm scarred." Sobs started to fill her. "After all that monster did to me, he's managed to take any chance of happiness away from me."

"Scarred?" Liz put her hand on Sadie's. "Tell me exactly what the doctor said."

"That the adhesions could make it difficult for me to get pregnant. She wants to do a laparoscopy to get a better look."

"When?" Liz asked her.

"I cancelled it," Sadie whispered.

"Sadie Lynn! Why did you do that?"

"He was already gone. I don't think I want to know the truth." Sadie stared down at her hands.

"He was perfect, Sadie."

"Exactly. He was perfect, and I'm so…."

"Broken?" Liz offered.

"Yes." Forever broken into pieces, that was the life she had left.

"Oh, Sadie. There were so many other options you had available. You should have talked about them with him." Liz gathered her in her arms.

"I was afraid." As much as she wanted to say she was protecting him, Sadie knew that her defense mechanisms had thrown up a wall to protect herself. She wasn't just keeping him from misery, she was preventing her happiness.

"I know. Have you tried talking to him?"

"He told me if I ran, he would not chase after me." Sadie refused to tell her about the texts in her phone. She didn't want Liz to push the issue with her. She needed to get her on board with the course Sadie had chosen.

"If he loves you, he'll always come," she reminded her. "The best ones do. When we want them to give up on us, they never do."

"If he loves me, he will stay away, Liz." Sadie started to cry all over again.

"That's it, time for some ice cream."

"No thank you." Sadie put a hand up.

"No ice cream? There's always room for ice cream."

The mere thought of ice cream made Sadie sick, like sour milk swirling in her stomach. "No…you can have some if you want. I'll pass."

"Fine, but you need to eat something. Crap!" Liz glanced down at her phone. "I have to get home. Something about a marble. How does that kid always find something to stick in an orifice?"

Sadie gave her a weak smile. "I'm okay."

"Like hell you are, but we'll revisit that. Tomorrow."

Sadie got up to let her out and locked the door behind her.

She knew Liz was right, she should eat something, but Sadie just couldn't bring herself to do that. Curling up on the couch, she hugged the pillow tightly against her and the tears fell once again. To love was to hurt. Sadie was so tired of being hurt. She knew she was not the victim here, but she fell into the why me's of life and wallowed deeper inside.

The next morning, she woke up and her stomach hurt painfully. She realized she was hungry, but very little sounded good. Making herself a glass of milk, she drank it slowly, for if she took it in too fast, she didn't think it would stay down. She followed it up with a slice of bacon, but that was painful to swallow. It made her think of the time that he had made breakfast here for her. She choked over it through her tears, swallowing it the best that she could. Gasping for breath, she slammed her fist on the counter. She saw her phone light up and wanted to reach for it so bad that her heart nearly leapt out of her chest, but she forced herself to stay the course.

The doorbell rang and she crept towards it, ignoring the phone that continued to make noise on the counter. She opened it to find Liz standing there with a bag of food.

"Out of the way. If you're not going to feed yourself, then I'll have to do it."

"I ate," she argued feebly.

"What?"

"Half a piece of bacon." Her eye shoulders shrugged slightly.

Liz tisked at her. "Sit down."

Sadie sat down at the table, staring at her hands. She did not see Liz checking her phone when it dinged again.

"Sadie Lynn! You told me he wasn't chasing you."

"He's not."

"Then why is he sending messages to you?"

"I keep hoping he will stop." It was true, but at the same time she lived for those messages. The day they stopped, that was the day everything would evaporate around her.

Liz was looking at her with concern. "You okay, Sadie? You don't look so good."

"I'm fine." She tried to stand up, but the world shifted around her.

"You look pale. Have you been to a doctor lately?" Liz asked her.

Sadie barely heard her words as she blinked against the wave of dizziness that took over. The world went black and grey as it swirled around her. "I don't feel so good."

It was the last thing she said before her body hit the floor. As she was in and out of consciousness, she was vaguely aware of Liz calling for assistance. Sadie tried to tell her not to make a big deal, that she was all right, but no words left her mouth. She watched as Liz let the EMTs into her apartment. Unable to respond to their questions, Sadie was in and out of consciousness, and her head hurt so bad she could barely think.

Chapter 22

Sadie was in and out of the darkness. She slept more than she was awake. She heard the blip of the machines near her bed. At one point she thought she heard a familiar voice threatening the nurses to let him in.

"Are you family?" A woman had asked him.

"That's my fiancé."

Sadie sighed, even in her sleep, when she heard Liz talking over all of them. "He's family."

That was the last thing she heard for awhile, but even in her sleep she felt her hand being pulled into his. It brought her a peace she had not felt in weeks.

"Is she going to be okay?" Justin asked Liz.

"I hope so. She was not in a good state." Liz sounded so cryptic.

"What did the doctor say?" Justin asked her.

"Dehydration, malnutrition, and…. Well…maybe you should wait to hear the rest. We're just waiting on her to wake up."

Justin put his lips on her hand and her fingers twitched slightly. "Do you think she knows we're here?"

"Yes. She's in and out. I think once she gets some nutrition in, she'll be okay."

"Thank you for calling me. I've been trying to—"

"I know. She's a tough cookie, Justin. She'll push you away twice as hard when all she wants to do is pull you closer. We're not easy creatures to live with." Liz smiled softly.

"How long have you known her?" Justin asked.

"Since college. We've got more in common than most people ever will. Our skeletons line up perfectly, if you get my drift." Liz took a breath. "There's nothing I wouldn't do to protect her, even if it means protecting her from herself. You?"

"I've known her all my life." His hand gripped hers harder, as if he were begging her to not ever let go of him.

Liz whistled. "You do have it bad."

"No one has ever measured up to her. No one ever could." He sighed.

"She has a lot of demons."

"I know all about them." He held his chin up. "I'm not afraid of a little work."

"Good. She's been working hard enough on her own for too long. She needs you."

"The funny thing is, I need her *more*."

Sadie's eyelids fluttered slightly. She had a vague recollection of what was happening around her. When she moved her head to see him holding her hand, tears gathered in her eyes. She was frozen in the moment, trying to gather a voice she could not bring forward.

"Eh hem. Well, I think I need a potty break. I'll be back in a little bit." When Justin turned to look at Liz, she nodded her head toward Sadie.

"Sadie...."

"Justin?" Her eyes were still trying to come into focus.

"It's okay, I'm here," he told her. He looked as if he had not slept in days.

"Why?" She closed her eyes and turned her head.

"Don't do that, Sadie."

"What?" she whispered.

"Turn away from me. Please, look at me," he begged her.

Sadie turned to look at him, planning on asking him to leave, but the doctor pulled the curtain back. "Ms. Turner, good. Glad to see you waking up. You gave us quite the scare. But it looks like you and the baby are doing just fine."

Sadie blinked. "I'm sorry. What did you say?"

"Well, it's still quite early, and it might be a bumpy road for you, considering the adhesions. Your friend mentioned those, so we did an exam."

Sadie was still confused. It was like he was speaking German to her. She withdrew inside herself, refusing to believe what he'd said. It was a cruel joke, a nightmare. She was probably still asleep, trapped in one nightmare or another.

"With the proper rest and nutrition, you should be right on course. Check in with your gynecologist. With your history, you might be at risk, so we'll need to keep a close eye on you."

When Sadie said nothing, Justin stepped in. "Thank you. We'll make sure."

As the doctor left, Sadie burst into tears. No, this could

not be happening. She cried so hard she couldn't seem to catch her breath, and almost started hyperventilating. When he reached for her hand she tried to push him away. She heard him let out a loud breath.

"Damn it, Sadie."

He pushed the rail of her bed down and fought her hands away as he climbed in next to her. The minute he cradled her body next to his, she relaxed against him. Even here, in the chaos of the busy hospital with the blipping of the machines and the bustling of everyone around them, the safety of his arms was like a lifeline she had never had before. The tears kept falling, but they hurt a little less.

Justin stroked her hair and whispered to her. "It's going to be all right, Sadie. It's all going to be all right."

Sleep beckoned her. She was so tired of fighting everything. All she wanted to do was lay there in his arms, no matter what happened next. She relaxed against him and sighed in contentment.

"That's my girl," he whispered as he kissed her cheek.

She barely heard Liz return. Justin was no longer in bed with her. Instead he was sitting next to her with his head in his hands.

"I take it you found out about the baby."

"Yes."

"How'd she take it?"

"I'm still trying to figure that one out." He sounded concerned. "I thought she wanted kids, but she seemed so devastated."

"Ah, well, I know this is her place to tell you, but I think she's been through enough of self-flatulation to last her a lifetime. So, if it's okay with you, I'm going to be her voice."

"Go on." His voice was barely audible.

"Since she met you, she's been trying to find a way to make herself fit into the life you want."

"She doesn't have to change." Justin's voice grated.

"No...she does. If you had gone through it, you would know. To have a healthy life, you have to be whole. She was working on that. She saw a counselor and made a healthy plan. Then she saw her ob/gyn, who put the idea in her head that she might not be able to have children, due to the asshole who destroyed her childhood."

Justin let out a loud breath. "Why didn't she tell me?"

"You painted a beautiful picture," Liz pointed out.

"This happened right before.... God, it all makes sense." Justin swore under his breath. "And then my sister told her about Nikki."

"Yep," Liz said matter-of-factly.

"No wonder."

"You can open your eyes now, Sadie."

Sadie tried to sink into the pillows. She had taken the coward's way out. She had heard Liz start to tell him everything she was terrified to voice. Sadie did open her eyes, but she refused to look over at them.

"I think I'm going to give you some more time. Plus, my cankles are starting to bother me."

"Cankles?" Justin asked in confusion as Liz waddled away. "Sadie?"

Sadie refused to look at him. How could she? She had been such an idiot, and put him through more than any person should. If she saw the absolution on his face, she would never be able to stop crying.

"Sadie Turner, you are not a coward. Look at me."

She bit her lip and turned to face him. "I'm—"

"The most frustrating, nerve wracking, confusing woman I have ever met. And I am always going to be here no matter how many pieces you break into. Every…single…time." The love in his eyes nearly destroyed her.

"I don't deserve you," she whispered.

"No…you don't. You deserve so much more."

She blinked. "But you are everything I've ever wanted."

"Say it again."

"What?"

"That you love me."

"But I didn't say that."

"Didn't you?"

"*I love you.*" Tears started to fill her eyes.

"I love you, every piece of you, Sadie. I don't need anything or anyone else to love you just the way you are."

"What if…?"

"No more what ifs. No tomorrows. Only todays. One step at a time. Got it?"

Sadie tried to sit up, but the minute she did she felt sick to her stomach. What was wrong with her? Then she remembered the words the doctor had said. "We're having a baby?"

"Yes…." He answered her tentatively, as if trying to determine how that knowledge made her feel.

"Seriously?"

"Uhh…yeah."

She teared up again. "That's the most wonderful thing

I've heard in days. Only one thing would make me happier."

"What's that?"

"Will you marry me?" she whispered, her eyes searching his for any kind of reaction.

He cleared his throat before he responded, his eyes seeming to water slightly. "I'll have to check my schedule."

"Why? We've got plenty of time to plan a wedding."

"Wedding?" His eyebrow rose.

"Yes. If we don't have a wedding, Liz will literally bludgeon me with a spork."

"A what?"

"A spork. I think she put it in her purse to save just in case."

"Hmm. What did they give you?" He asked her.

Sadie giggled. "It's called love. I'm drowning in it."

Justin climbed into bed and pulled her against him. "I want you more than the air I breathe, Sadie."

"Me too," she sighed against him. Sadie knew that she was where she wanted to be. He was home, and she would never run from him again.

Chapter 23

A year later...

The sun shone down on the beach before her, as Sadie made her way down the sandy path that led her to the only place she ever wanted to be, solidified together for eternity. If anyone had told her she would walk this road years ago, Sadie would have told them they had lost their minds. But here she was in a white dress that floated around her like a dream.

She saw the loved ones who had gathered near, the family she had gained over the past year. His parents had come back from Australia to see their son finally marry the love of his life, and to meet the new joy that had been brought into their lives. Sadie could hear them calling her from here and felt her chest tighten painfully.

"Ouch," she muttered.

"Did you put the breast pads in?" Liz teased her from in front of her.

"Yes. I'm not sure it will be enough, though." Any time she heard a baby cry, her boobs seemed to cry in reflex.

"Good thing you went with white," she teased her.

"Shut it, Liz!"

"Smile, or they'll think you're going to run away," Liz told her pointedly.

"I couldn't run if I wanted to. And I don't want to. Not ever again."

"Good girl. Now, let's get this show on the road."

Sadie followed Liz to the end of the row, and paused when she saw Justin. The look on his face took her breath away. She was his beacon, the lighthouse leading him in from the shores, just as he was for her. They were made for each other. Stepping closer, she paused only to stop and kiss the child in his mother's arms. Then she turned to the one cradled in Claire's too.

Finding out that she was pregnant had been a shock, but it was the day the ultrasound had revealed two little peanuts nestled inside that had nearly sent Justin into overdrive. He had been overprotective at times, to the point where she had to throw the nearest non-damaging item at him. At other times, he had been a constant reminder of the love she would always know by his side.

She walked up to the altar, where the officiant started with her opening words. "Love is patient, love is...."

Everything she'd never dreamed it could be. And so much more.

About the Author

Ever since childhood, Elissa Daye has enjoyed reading stories as an escape from life. When she was a teenager she started to write her own stories that kept her entertained when she ran out of books to read. When she was accepted into Illinois Summer School for the Arts in her Junior year of High School, she knew she wanted to become a writer. Elissa graduated from Illinois State University in December 1999 with a Bachelor of Science in Elementary Education and began her teaching career, hoping to find moments to write in her free time.

After seven years of teaching, Elissa decided to focus on her writing and made the decision to put her teaching years behind her so that she could create the stories she had always dreamed of. She is now happily married and a stay at home mom, who writes in every spare moment she can find, doing her best to master the art of multitasking to get everything accomplished.

CPSIA information can be obtained
at www.ICGtesting.com
Printed in the USA
BVHW031047220519
548904BV00025B/68/P